"You're looking  **said, as much f** **"I want to settle**

"Sounds like we're headed in different directions."

"I'm afraid so."

She expected him to pull away. Thought that he'd come to the same realization that they were wrong for one another. When he didn't move, she decided she'd have to be the one to leave. To march into the kitchen and put the finishing touches on the cake she'd started. It was what any smart, sane person would do.

Unfortunately, smart wasn't exactly how she felt sitting next to Colt in the middle of the night in a house where the only other living being was a four-year-old sound asleep upstairs. Hungry, maybe. And not for dessert. His touch stirred a visceral response, one that had everything to do with wanting the big rancher's arms around her, his lips pressed against hers.

Dear Reader,

When I told my cousin Paula Crews I was writing a book set in south Florida, she invited me to her ranch outside of Okeechobee. Since that day, Paula has generously shared her knowledge of ranching, but it was her note that inspired me to write *The Bull Rider's Family*.

I can't tell you how many times I have looked at a sunrise or a sunset, looked at the trees when the light is golden, and thanked God...that I have had this opportunity in life. Watching the wind dance across a field of fresh, tall, green grass while I am standing in my pasture surrounded by cattle, listening to them pulling the grass and eating—there is no sight, smell or sound like it. The smell of a horse, the leather of your saddle and the feel of that horse under you are things you will never forget. I am truly blessed.

Emma Shane also knows very little about ranching when she reports for her new job as cook on the Circle P. Before long, though, more than soup simmers in the kitchen as fourth-generation rancher Colt Judd tempts Emma to take a chance on a former rodeo star whose tumbleweed existence threatens the stability she craves.

I loved writing *The Bull Rider's Family* and hope you enjoy reading Emma and Colt's story. Thanks to Paula, it is far better than it might have been. Thanks, too, for the support of my Writers Camp pals Roxanne St. Claire, Kristen Painter and Lara Santiago.

Leigh

THE BULL RIDER'S FAMILY

—

LEIGH DUNCAN

HARLEQUIN® AMERICAN ROMANCE®

Recycling programs
for this product may
not exist in your area.

ISBN-13: 978-0-373-75521-9

THE BULL RIDER'S FAMILY

Copyright © 2014 by Linda Duke Duncan

Printed in U.S.A.

ABOUT THE AUTHOR

Bestselling author Leigh Duncan writes the kind of books she loves to read—ones where home, family and community are key to the happy endings we all deserve. Married to the love of her life and mother of two wonderful young adults, Leigh lives on central Florida's east coast.

When she isn't busy working on her next story for Harlequin American Romance, Leigh loves nothing better than to curl up in her favorite chair with a cup of hot coffee and a great book. She invites readers to follow her on Twitter, @leighrduncan, or visit her Facebook page, at www.facebook.com/LeighDuncanBooks. Contact her at P.O. Box 410787, Melbourne, FL 32941, or visit her online at www.leighduncan.com.

Books by Leigh Duncan

HARLEQUIN AMERICAN ROMANCE

1304—THE OFFICER'S GIRL
1360—THE DADDY CATCH
1406—RODEO DAUGHTER
1431—RANCHER'S SON
1488—SECOND CHANCE FAMILY

For Emma Elizabeth,
who fills every dish with laughter and love.

Chapter One

"Are we there yet, Mommy?"

Emma Shane slowly counted to ten when her daughter's sneakered foot struck the side of her seat. Again. Strapping her four-year-old into the center of the car offered the best protection but, apparently, none of the safety experts had considered the added wear and tear on a mother's nerves. Emma craned her neck until she met a pair of dark eyes in the rearview mirror.

"Don't kick, Bree." Summoning patience she certainly hadn't learned at her own mother's knee, she spoke softly. "Want a juice box?" At Bree's nod, Emma reached into a stash nearly depleted after two days on the road.

"Are we there, Mom?"

"Not quite, honey, but we're getting close."

Emma swept the back of her hand across her face. Late spring in Florida was more intense than she'd expected, but the perspiration that dampened her brow had more to do with second thoughts than her car's faltering air conditioner. Still, sweat was sweat. She wiped her hand on her jeans while she prayed that this time she'd made the right decision. That this move would be their last. She spared a quick glance at the hand-drawn map taped to the dashboard.

"Real close," she added.

Twenty miles outside of Okeechobee. Two miles past the abandoned gas station on the right. She counted five driveways after the blinking yellow caution light. At number six, she signaled for a left turn and braked to let an approaching semi pass.

Emma gripped the steering wheel, her car swaying while the truck thundered by. Vents in the carrier's long sides provided a quick glimpse of cattle on their way to market, proof there was more to Florida than citrus, beaches and tourist attractions.

She glanced at the scenery that hadn't varied since she'd turned inland from the coast three hours ago. Under a sun so bright it washed the color out of the sky, cows dotted the pale green grass that stretched as far as she could see. Ahead, shimmering mirages wavered on the blacktop. She squinted, making sure no other vehicles approached.

The way clear, Emma pulled across the two-lane road onto a dirt apron beneath a sign that was surprisingly nondescript considering the idyllic pictures on the Circle P's website. She stopped to get her bearings and stared at a graveled track that stretched into the utterly flat distance before it disappeared around a copse of low trees.

Had she made yet another wrong turn in a life filled with them?

The wide gate, according to the directions included in the folder along with her job offer, absolutely had to remain closed at all times. Someone had propped the gate to one side. They'd even looped the security chain around a post, making sure it stayed that way.

If this was the Circle P's version of a welcome mat, it wasn't much of one.

Thud. Bree's sneaker struck Emma's seat again. "Mommy…"

The symbol branded into the wooden sign overhead confirmed that, locked gate or not, they were in the right place. Emma brushed the end of a long ponytail over one shoulder.

"The main house and the barn should be just another half mile ahead. Help me look for them, okay, kiddo?"

She put the vehicle in gear. When gravel shifted and spit from beneath the sedan's tires, she slowed the car to a crawl.

"Look, Mommy! There's cows. Lots of them. Where are the horses? Can I have a horse, Mommy? And cowboy boots. And a cowboy hat. Can I, Mom? Huh? Huh?"

"We'll see." Emma stared at the sharp horns sported by several dozen cattle. Her gaze dropped to the strands of thin wire strung between wooden posts. As she had a dozen times during the long drive, she wondered if walking away from all she'd worked for in the four years since Jack's death had been her best idea. She shook her head.

Going back was not an option.

She'd reduced that particular bridge to ash when, in the middle of yet another of Chef Larue's nightly meltdowns, she'd rolled her knives into their carrying case. Hung her apron on a hook by the door. Emptied out her locker. And walked out on the belligerent cook, leaving him with no one to scream at but the busboys.

Maybe she shouldn't have, but Seth's job offer had given her the courage to leave. Really, though, Chef Larue shared the blame. He'd set things in motion by putting her in charge of catering the Cattlemen's Association awards dinner, where she'd met Seth and Doris Judd.

Emma had instantly warmed to the soft-spoken older couple, who'd raved about the bite-size beef taco appetizers, a recipe she'd created especially for the event. They'd talked for hours, Seth and Doris sharing stories that made life on the ranch he managed in southern Florida sound absolutely perfect. When the wizened ranch hand had asked her to recommend a place for their wedding anniversary, Emma had slipped him a card, good for two complimentary dinners at the tony Chez Larue. Two nights later, she'd joined them at their table.

In his thank-you note, Seth suggested she leave New York's frenetic pace behind and come to the Circle P as his wife's assistant. Though she wasn't quite ready to make that change, Emma had considered the offer each time Chef Larue rapped his famed wooden spoon across the fingers of an error-prone line cook. She'd weighed the merits of idyllic ranch life whenever she slogged through ice and snow on her way to the bus stop. Or when the babysitter didn't show up, or Bree brought another cold home from day care. Until, finally, she'd asked Seth to put the details in writing.

The day the offer arrived in the mail, her fingers had shaken so badly she had to read the contract twice before she understood that Seth was handing her the opportunity to run her own kitchen—after a short apprenticeship. The deal included a house, hers as long as she stayed on the ranch. Finally, she could provide Bree with the safe, secure childhood Emma had yearned for since she was her daughter's age.

Okay, maybe she should have looked a little closer at the picture Seth and his wife, Doris, had painted of the

Circle P. From behind the wheel of her car, she studied the road that seemed to lead to nowhere. The setting was far more rustic, far more isolated, than she'd ever dreamed. She wished she'd thought to ask for photos of the kitchen and cringed imagining rust-coated refrigerators and warped counters.

Her neck stiffened, and she rolled it.

Accurate image or not, there was no turning back. For both their sakes—hers and Bree's—she had to make this work. She'd learn a new style of cooking, prove she could run a kitchen that catered to both ranch hands and the Circle P's upscale clientele. And she'd do it in the year before Doris retired.

She filled her lungs. With two years of culinary school and another couple as a sous chef under her belt, she was ready for the challenge.

The highway disappeared from her rearview mirror as the long driveway curved around the trees. Emerging on the far side, Emma held her breath and braced for her first glimpse of their new home. Her foot eased off the gas. The car rolled to a stop while she studied an immaculate two-story house. An impressive barn occupied the space to one side. Opposite it stood a gigantic greenhouse. But the biggest surprise were the cars and pickup trucks. Dozens of them. They haphazardly crowded a grassless yard between the buildings.

"Mommy, is there a party?" Bree unsnapped her seat belt the second Emma found a spot wide enough to accommodate her compact car. "Can we have cake?"

"Even if there is a party," Emma cautioned, "we weren't invited." Despite Seth's assurances that family came first on the Circle P, learning how much the hired help mingled with the guests was on her lengthy to-do list.

Stepping from the car, Emma fanned air so thick with moisture her shirt instantly clung to her skin. Before she'd taken two steps, the jeans she'd worn while driving tugged uncomfortably at her waist, her knees. Knowing she'd need all the help she could get to project an image of poise and self-confidence when she met her new employers, she reached past Bree and tugged the jacket of her chef's whites from its hanger.

"Mommy, what stinks?" Bree scrambled from her car seat, her nose wrinkling.

Emma gave a cautious sniff. A dank undertone floated in the breathless air. "Smells like cows," she said. Well, what did she expect? They were on a cattle ranch, after all.

She slid her arms into the snug uniform. From the trunk, she took the basket of cookies and other baked goods she'd carefully wrapped to withstand their twelve-hundred-mile journey.

"Are you ready?" She ran a smoothing hand over Bree's dark curls. "You remember everything I told you?"

Bree nodded all too solemnly for a preschooler. "No running in the house. No yelling. Mrs. Wickles and me, we'll be good." Bree squeezed her much-loved doll to her chest. "Won't we, Mrs. Wickles?"

Emma shrugged. Having her active daughter underfoot in the kitchen was asking for trouble, but what choice did she have? She and Bree were on their own in the world. They were venturing into new territory. They'd have to find their way.

She gave Bree an extra-reassuring hug.

"Okay, then," she said at last.

Hand in hand, they crossed the open yard to a narrow strip of lawn. The temperature dropped ten degrees as they mounted the steps onto the shaded porch. At regular intervals, waxy flowering plants hung from the eaves. Emma drank in the sweet scent that overpowered the odor of manure. At the massive entryway, she squared her shoulders. Poised to knock, Emma quickly nudged Bree out of the way when the door sprang wide.

A tall, masculine figure brushed past. Emma caught the barest glimpse of a chiseled jaw before the man stopped at the edge of the porch to tug a black cowboy hat low over thick dark hair.

"Excuse me." She juggled the heavy basket at her hip. "Do you know where I might find Mr. Judd?"

The stranger frowned. "You'll have to be a bit more specific. There's six—" An odd expression twisted his lips. "Five," he corrected. "There's five of us."

Though his high cheekbones and sculpted nose reminded Emma of Seth Judd's, this man's expression appeared to be carved into a permanent scowl. One that deepened as ice-blue eyes scoured her jacket.

"Deliveries go round to the back," he said sharply.

Without another word, he spun away, his boots ringing against the wide wooden planks as he stalked down the stairs. In an obvious move to put as much distance between them as possible, he strode across the yard toward the barn.

So much for Southern hospitality, Emma thought while she stared at a pair of wide shoulders that tapered to slim hips. Bree tugged on her hand.

"Mommy," she whispered, her eyes nearly as wide as her mouth. "Was he a real cowboy?"

"I'm not sure, baby," she answered. Neither Seth nor Doris had mentioned having a grown son, but then, their descriptions of the Circle P hadn't mentioned the half-hour drive between the ranch and the closest town.

She squeezed her daughter's hand. "Come on, honey," she whispered. "Let's go see if we can find the kitchen."

With a final glance toward the barn, she led the way around the corner, not stopping till they reached a small concrete patio shaded by an oak tree that towered over the house. There, two young men sat eating lunch at one of several picnic tables that dotted another patch of lawn.

Emma mustered a bright smile. "I'm Emma Shane." She tugged Bree forward. "This is my daughter, Bree."

One of the lanky young men half rose. "I'm Tim," he said, extending a work-hardened hand. "He's Christopher."

"Chris," the second boy corrected. "You dropping something off for the funeral?" He peered expectantly at the basket Emma held.

Funeral. Whose?

Recalling the cowboy's odd reference, Emma swallowed. "I'm supposed to see Mr. Judd. Mr. Seth Judd. Is he around?"

Sorrow shimmered in Tim's brown eyes. "Mr. Seth? He died."

"He's…dead?" Emma blinked. Nausea rolled through her stomach. "How? When?"

"Three days ago." Chris spoke around the bite of pie he'd just forked into his mouth. "The service was this morning." He gestured toward the main house. "Everybody's come to pay their respects."

"Mommy, you're holding me too tight," Bree protested.

"Sorry, baby." Despite the fresh beads of perspiration that broke across her brow, Emma loosened her grip. She sipped air and tried to figure out what to do next. Had she come all this way for nothing? The job offer was in her folder, the contracts to be signed upon her arrival. Surely Seth's replacement would honor their deal.

"Do you work here? In the kitchen?"

"In the greenhouse mostly," Tim answered.

"Sometimes we wash dishes," Chris added.

"I'm Ms. Judd's new assistant," Emma said, once more extending her hand to first Tim and then Chris. She paused when the boys stared at her as if she was some alien life-form. But until she could speak with Doris, or whoever was in charge, she'd been hired to do a job. There was no time like the present to start it.

At last, Tim shrugged. "Ms. Doris, she's busy right now."

Emma's chest tightened. Memories of the days immediately after Jack's death flooded back, and with them, the overwhelming sense of loss. "I'm sure she is," she murmured. "So why don't you tell me a little bit about yourselves, and then we'll see what we need to do next."

Tim and Chris, it turned out, had bounced around the foster care system until the owners of the Circle P took them under their wings. Free to go wherever they wanted once they turned eighteen, they'd decided to stay on at the ranch in hopes of learning a trade. Today, that meant washing dishes.

"Well, I'm sure Doris'll appreciate your being here," Emma said.

Their introductions complete, she eased open the screened door and shepherded her daughter inside. Longing swept through her as she surveyed the spacious kitchen. Ignoring the dirty dishes and items that cluttered every surface, she focused on granite counters and high ceilings. She drank in the light that poured through windows over the sink. Contrary to her worst fears, not a speck of rust dotted the twin Sub-Zero refrigerators and freezers built into one wall. Opposite them, an enormous AGA stove glistened beneath a pile of pots and pans.

Eager to get to work, she flexed her fingers. Though the kitchen wasn't perfect, it had definite possibilities. But Seth's death complicated things, and she swallowed a twinge of concern as she cleared a space for her basket on one of the counters. She glanced pointedly toward an enormous sink.

"Tim, why don't you and Chris start washing dishes while I get some of this food organized." She took a second look, noting a wealth of plastic-wrapped platters on the long trestle table and some of the counters. "Where did all this come from?"

"No one shows up to a funeral empty-handed." Chris shrugged.

Tim nodded. "There's plenty more when the food on the buffet is gone. I been stickin' casseroles in the fridge, but it's full."

She hiked an eyebrow. Thinking of potato salad and meats left too long at room temperature, Emma stifled a groan.

Tomorrow, she'd figure out where she and Bree would go from here and whether the new boss would honor her arrangement with Seth. But for now, there was a kitchen to run and, although the circumstances were far from what she'd expected, she intended to give it her best shot.

His Sunday Stetson clamped firmly on his head, Colt Judd let his long strides take him wherever they wanted. He wasn't a bit surprised when they stopped at the empty pen where he'd ridden his first bull. He propped his elbows against the top rail and stared, unseeing, at the ranch his father had spent an entire life managing.

He wasn't sure how long he stood there before the scuff of another pair of boots broke the late afternoon stillness.

"Thought I'd find you out here. You hanging in there?"

At the familiar voice, Colt squared his shoulders. "I'm all right," he managed despite an unmanly tightness in his throat. "Just needed a breath of fresh air."

He'd had to leave the house. Had to get away. Away from the friends he hadn't seen in so long they were practically strangers. From the cloying scent of hothouse flowers. From the clink of ice in a dozen glasses.

If he had to endure the carefully guarded conversations in the great room another second, he'd implode. He knew he would. He'd seen the censure in the eyes of every person who'd gathered to pay their respects. Even though, so far, no one had been brave enough—or foolish enough—to say it, behind their sympathetic words, he knew they blamed him.

And rightly so. His father's death was his fault.

He should have hung up his spurs after winning a second gold buckle in Vegas three years ago. Should have come home, instead of signing on as the Professional Bull Riders' advance man. Should have known there was more to his dad's frequent reminders that there was always a place for him on the Circle P.

He should have. He could have. He hadn't.

If he'd simply said *I'm on my way* instead of heading to Tulsa the last time they spoke, he could have eased his dad's workload. Maybe then, grave diggers wouldn't be lowering his father's casket into a hole six feet deep.

At the image, Colt bit back the urge to howl.

"Tell me about it." Ty Parker folded his arms across a nearby post. "I was the same way when Dad passed."

Colt scuffed one dress boot through the gray sand. It hadn't been so long ago that his boyhood pal lost his own father. Now Ty owned the ranch where Colt and all four of his brothers had been born and raised.

"Hard to believe he's gone. Every time I turn a corner, I expect to run into him. He was always there." Tears clogged his throat. Colt coughed and changed the subject. "Can we use your office in a bit? We've got some family business to discuss before everybody heads out in another day or so. Garrett plans to ask Mom to visit him and Arlene for a while."

Out of the corner of one eye, he saw Ty flinch.

"The Circle P might not survive losing both your folks," his friend offered. "There's been a Judd here as long as there've been Parkers."

Colt nodded. He'd grown up on stories of the ranch and the two families whose lives were deeply entwined. Four generations of Parkers had owned the Circle P. Four generations of Judds had managed its thousands of acres and the cattle that roamed them. He shrugged one shoulder. "Gotta do whatever Mom wants. No matter what she chooses, the next few months are gonna be hard enough for her."

Ty's long exhale filled the gap in the conversation. "Guess I'd better tell Sarah that month in Hawaii she's got her heart set on is gonna have to wait…again."

"You never did get to take that trip, did you?" Colt squinted at his friend. "What happened last time? Mom told me but, for the life of me, I can't remember the details." Or much else he'd heard ever since the phone call that had summoned him home three days earlier.

Ty's mouth slanted to one side. "Jimmy came down with chicken pox on Christmas Day. I couldn't get Sarah to leave him." He chuckled. "Not even when I promised to let her take me skinny dippin' in the ocean."

Two years had passed since then, but Colt barely raised an eyebrow at the delayed honeymoon. Ranching was more than a full-time job. It was a lifestyle. One that didn't come with vacation or sick days.

"Hold off on changing your plans for a bit. The boys and I—we're working on a way to help out. We just have to clear things with Mom first."

"Doris can be a mite stubborn." Ty resettled his own Stetson. "Whatever she decides, Colt, we'll muddle through. But the Circle P will never be the same without your dad."

That damned tightness filled his throat again, but Colt managed an abrupt, "I hear ya," before it closed completely.

Fifteen minutes later, he placed his hand on his mom's shoulder and winced at the unexpected thinness of arms that had always seemed sturdy. Strands of gray hair had worked loose from her thick, trademark braid. Wisps brushed against the back of his wrist, but Doris made no effort to push them back behind her ears. He resisted an urge to do it for her and gave his mom a closer look.

Had she really aged twenty years in the past week? Or had he been too busy living his own life to notice his parents' silvered hair and slower steps? He mopped his face with one hand while another twinge of guilt struck him in the gut.

In the office, Colt settled his mom into the big wing chair beside Ty's desk. Crossing to the large picture window, he leaned against the frame while his brothers filed in to take their places. Long, lean and nearly as tall as Colt, Hank perched on the edge of another chair while Garrett stood in front of the fireplace as if he were at the head of the class and not just the oldest of Seth and Doris's five sons. As usual, Randy and Royce claimed the places closest to Doris. The youngest of the Judds, the twins had been the last to strike out from the Circle P on their own and, while the older siblings absorbed their father's death with outward stoicism, the stocky twenty-four-year-olds weren't as good at hiding their emotions.

The designated leader, Garrett rapped his knuckles on the mantel. "Mom, we're all sticking around for another day or two," he began once the room quieted. "We can talk tomorrow if you're not up to this."

In a voice so slight Colt had to lean forward to catch it, Doris answered, "Might as well get started. We have plans to make."

Colt frowned when the hands that had put breakfast on the table every one of his thirty-two years plucked uselessly at a wrinkle in her skirt.

"Your dad, he loved each one of you so much. I don't know how any of us will get along without him."

Five sturdy men reached for the nearest tissue box when eyes the same blue as their own filled with tears. To her credit, Doris pulled herself together much quicker than Colt thought he was capable of doing.

Scanning the young men gathered round her, she continued. "But I do know I can't stay here. I can't work in that kitchen, can't sleep in our bed. I'll expect him to walk through the door the minute I take the biscuits out of the oven. Or show up for supper at six every night. I need to get away for a bit."

Randy broke in. "But where will—"

"—you go, Mom?" Royce finished the question.

From his perch by the window, Colt hid a smile. He doubted either of the twins had ever finished a single sentence on their own.

Doris studied the end of the braid she'd twisted around one finger. "I might go see my sister."

His mom wasn't thinking straight and a survey of the frowns on his brothers' faces only confirmed it. Doris and Aunt Tilly had never gotten along. A fact borne out by Tilly's absence from today's funeral. Colt shot Garrett a questioning look.

The senior Judd cleared his throat. "Arlene wanted to be here for you. She was pretty broken up that she couldn't come with me. The pregnancy's been hard on her, and her doctor won't let her travel." He exhaled slowly. "He wants her to rest as much as possible."

Worry lines creased Garrett's brow. Colt grimaced as more guilt tore through his midsection. For too long he'd ignored the little voice in the back of his head telling him to go home.

His older brother turned an unsteady look on their mom. "We could sure use your help. That is, if your mind's not set on going to California."

The heartfelt plea stirred the first sign of life Colt had seen on his mom's face since he'd arrived at the Circle P. He leaned forward.

Doris took a minute to consider. "You're sure Arlene won't feel I'm imposing?"

"It was her idea. You know how much she loves you." Along with half the kids in town, Arlene had practically grown up on the ranch.

Doris tucked her lower lip between her teeth, a move every one of her sons recognized as a sure sign that she was mulling things over. "What about things here?" she asked at last. "I feel bad leaving Ty and Sarah in the lurch."

Colt didn't need his brother's not-so-subtle nod to recognize his cue.

"Ranching is in our blood, thanks to you and Dad," he said. "We all know how things are done, how they're supposed to be done. Dad would have wanted us to carry on the tradition of working with the Parkers, always having a Judd on the Circle P. And every one of us would do it if we could."

Throughout the room, dark-haired men nodded in agreement.

"Royce and Randy, they've been hankering to come home for a while. But they're tied up in Montana till the first of the year."

Randy reached for his mom's arm. "We signed a contract with Mr. Sizemore."

"As soon as we fulfill it, we'll come back and run the Circle P," Royce finished.

Doris patted her youngest sons' hands. "That's good, boys. Your dad would be proud to have you take over." Her eyes sought Colt's. "But that's the better part of a year. Too long to leave the ranch without a manager."

Colt scanned the room and found the support he needed in eyes very much like his own.

"Garrett plans to teach summer school. Besides, with a baby on the way, it's not a good time for him and Arlene to move. Hank'd have to close his real estate office. That leaves me." He pulled his six-foot-three-inch frame erect and straightened his shoulders so his mom could see they were wide enough to carry the burdens of the Circle P. "I'll handle things here till Royce and Randy can."

Doris's eyes narrowed. "Are you sure, Colt?" she asked. "I thought your job with the PBR kept you pretty busy."

He tried not to react. After all, his mom had merely repeated the same words he'd been saying for far too long. That his job as the advance man for the Professional Bull Riders kept him busy. Too busy.

But he couldn't ignore the bitter truth any longer. He'd always taken his mom and his dad for granted. Never considered that, by the time he was ready to put down roots, they might not be around.

"I'll take a leave of absence. Already talked to my boss about it." He waved away the potent mix of gratitude and concern that shimmered in his mom's eyes. He let his voice drop. "Nothing's more important than you right now, Mom. If having me here will put you at ease, I'm proud to do it."

And after Randy and Royce took over, then what?

There were probably fifty guys who'd jump at the chance to fill his boots in the PBR. If one or two of them were good at getting things done, he might not have a job to go back to. He shook his head. His focus, now, had to be on his mom. And, though he'd be the first to point out that it was too little, too late, filling his dad's boots was the least he could do to make up for not being here when he was needed.

"Then it's settled?" Doris asked. "We'll talk to Ty and Sarah? Continue the Judd-Parker tradition?"

Colt stopped gathering wool long enough to agree. As the family filed out of the office a few minutes later, he felt a hand land firmly on his shoulder.

"This recession's put a serious dent in the real estate market. I'm working night and day to keep my office open." Hank pitched his voice low enough that no one else overheard. "But you say the word, Colt, and I'll be here. No matter what."

"Thanks, bro. I appreciate it." Colt clasped his brother's arm. "I'm gonna sit down with Ty tonight. He ought to be able to bring me up to speed before he and Sarah head to Hawaii. But, yeah, I'll call."

He watched his mom make her way through the great room that had emptied of neighbors while they'd been in the back talking. "You think she'll be all right?" he asked once she moved out of sight.

Hank cupped his chin in his hand. "She's tough. Anyone who ranches for a living has to be. But they were together for thirty-seven years. That's gotta leave a big hole."

Colt swallowed. Thirty-seven years. These days, not many couples stayed together half that long. Hank and his wife hadn't. That marriage had spiraled into so much bitterness his ex used their ten-year-old daughter as a bargaining chip.

His empty stomach rumbled, and he eyed the dining room. When they'd headed into the office, dishes of all kinds had crowded every inch of the long table. He'd been too keyed up to eat then. Now that things were more or less settled, he could use a little something but, as luck would have it, not a dish or a platter remained in sight.

"Guess I'd better head into the kitchen," he told Hank. "See if I can't rustle up a bite or two before dinner."

Leaving his brother to his own devices, Colt passed through the hallway where photographs recorded the long history of the Circle P. He stopped to tap his fingers on one taken of his dad and Tom Parker herding the ranch's famed Andalusian cattle across a narrow stream. He inhaled slowly and, on the exhale, vowed to continue their work, just as they'd done for their fathers.

His task set, his path determined, he continued on toward the kitchen. There, he stared in disbelief as a woman in white scraped the contents of an entire casserole pan into the trash can.

Tradition.

He'd sworn to uphold the Judd and Parker traditions. And from the time he'd been old enough to dish scrambled eggs from a platter, he'd been taught that wasting food was nearly a sin. He strode into the room, his voice rising.

"Stop that!"

The woman spun toward him, anger glittering in her dark eyes. "What gives you the right to walk into my kitchen, yelling and shouting orders?" she demanded.

Colt felt his eyebrows slam together. "Your kitchen?" This had been, and always would be, his mother's kitchen. "Look, lady, I don't know who hired you, but you're done. Write down your hours. I'll make sure you're paid for your time before you leave."

Something akin to fear flashed in the prettiest brown eyes he'd seen in a long time.

Damn.

He hadn't meant to scare her. He only wanted her to put things back the way they were.

Chapter Two

Emma swung toward the man who'd marched into the room barking orders like a general. Over a square chin, his full lips thinned. A muscle twitched between his sharply defined jaw and high cheekbones. Beneath hair the color of a starless night, icy blue eyes pinned her with a demanding glare.

She ripped her gaze away from all that anger and dark good looks to focus on Bree. Her little girl cowered on the stool, her face nearly as pale as her doll's. Emma hurried across the room. From the first moment she'd held her baby in her arms, she'd sworn she'd give her daughter a better childhood than the one she'd endured. One where people didn't shout or raise their fists to get their point across. No matter what.

"It's okay, baby," she cooed. She smoothed long tresses and felt her daughter shudder.

"That man scared Mrs. Wickles." Bree clung to her doll. "Why's he mad, Mama? Did I do something wrong?"

Why, indeed.

"No, honey. He's probably just having a bad day. Let me talk to him for a minute. We'll get this straightened out."

The cheery smile Emma forced to her lips didn't fool

Bree. Not for one second. The little girl shrank even smaller.

Watching her daughter cringe, Emma felt white heat lace through her midsection. She spun toward the stranger, staring up at the man whose size dwarfed her own five feet three inches. He had the audacity to stare back at her, his arms folded across a massive chest.

Well, if he thought he could get away with that in *her* kitchen, he'd better think again. As a child, she hadn't had a choice. She'd had to listen to her father rant and rave. Hoping to preserve her marriage, she'd tolerated her husband's my-way-or-the-highway attitude far longer than she should have. And yes, in choosing to work in an upscale restaurant, she'd traded one hostile environment for another.

But those days were over.

For her daughter's sake, for her own sanity, she was done with arrogant men. She'd go toe-to-toe with this one, and she'd do it on her terms. She sipped air.

"How dare you march in here full of vinegar and soda. Who do you think you are?" she demanded without raising her voice above a whisper.

"I'm the guy in charge. Now, pack your things and leave." A five o'clock shadow graced the chin he lifted to emphasize his point.

"I. Don't. Think. So." Emma plunged her fisted hands into the pockets of her chef's whites. She'd traveled twelve hundred miles to work here. To take over when Doris retired.

Beyond the doorway, footsteps hurried on the hall's tiled floor. A tired voice floated into the room. "Colt? Is everything all right?"

The man's blue eyes flashed a warning. Through

clenched teeth he said, "We aren't finished here, you and me."

"Everything's fine, Mom," he called over one shoulder. His posture softening, he turned toward the door behind him as a woman dressed in black stepped into view. The harshness faded from his tone. "I thought you were lying down."

Emma's brow furrowed. While her mind connected the dots, she glanced from Doris to the man who'd barged into the kitchen. The day a son buried his father was as bad as they came.

"I wanted a cup of tea first," Doris answered. Her watery blue eyes swept past Colt to land on Emma.

"Oh, my. Is it Friday already? Things have been a bit muddled since…" Doris stopped to take a breath. "These last few days." She twisted the rings on her left hand. The ghost of a smile deepened the wrinkles of her lined face. "Is this your daughter?" Her smile widened though the pain in her eyes remained. "She's adorable," she added at Bree's shy wave.

"She's my world," Emma acknowledged.

The faint tremble of age-spotted fingers summoned a rush of sympathy. Emma crossed to the newly bereaved widow.

"Doris, I only just heard the news. I'm so sorry about Seth. He was such a nice man. If there's anything I can do—" She blinked when sturdy arms reached past her extended hand to draw her into a warm embrace.

"You're already doing it by being here," Doris whispered.

A lump rose in Emma's throat. When Jack died, she'd have been lost without the friends who'd shown up bearing casseroles and sympathy. It was time to return the favor. She patted Doris's shoulder, waiting until the woman's firm grip eased before she slowly retreated.

After giving her eyes a quick swipe, Doris reached for her son's forearm.

"Colt, you've met Emma Shane."

"We haven't been formally introduced." His hands hung by his thumbs from the pockets of his Wranglers. "Colt Judd." He nodded. Without waiting for a response, he turned to his mother. "What's she doing here?"

"Don't be rude, dear." Doris tapped lightly on Colt's shoulder. "It took a fair amount of arm twisting to get Emma to leave Chef Larue and come to the Circle P. She's… She was going to learn how to take care of things here so your dad and I could retire."

"Retire?" Colt's blue eyes widened.

Doris nodded. "Time to pass the reins on to a new generation. We'd planned to talk to you and the rest of the boys about it one of these days." She straightened her shoulders. "Well. No time like the present."

Emma practically felt Colt's glance scour her white coat as the tension in the room ratcheted tighter. "We don't have much use for a fancy chef on the Circle P."

"Maybe. Maybe not." Doris sighed visibly. "But we have a lot of people to feed and, if memory serves me correctly, you're not going to be the one putting meals on the table. Not unless you've learned how to boil water in the years you've been away."

Beneath his deep tan, Colt blanched as if Doris had struck a mortal blow, but he didn't back down.

"I caught her throwing away perfectly good food."

"And I'm sure she had a reason." One gray brow rose expectantly over Doris's left eye.

Taking the hint, Emma found her voice. With more

control than she'd been tempted to show seconds earlier, she explained. "The dishes in the dining room had been out since noon. At least. Without refrigeration or heat, none of it was safe to eat. I thought we'd start fresh. There are casseroles in the oven, salads in the cooler. As soon as you give the word, Tim and Chris can help me replenish."

"That's just what I would have done." Doris turned to her son. "She knows what she's doing." When Colt still glowered, Doris's voice dropped. "Besides, your father thought Emma was perfect for the ranch. Her daughter, too."

Like a cake taken too early from the oven, Colt's bravado collapsed. His shoulders rounded though his mouth remained set in firm, no-nonsense lines.

"It seems I owe you an apology," he began.

Emma waited a half beat before deciding that Colt's remark was as close to an *I'm sorry* as he planned to deliver. She turned to Doris. "You wanted some tea, ma'am?"

"It can wait. We need to talk." Doris scrubbed her hands on her skirt. "I know we promised you a lengthy internship while you learned the ropes here at the Circle P, but my husband's death…" Her voice trailed off.

To his credit, Colt slung an arm around his mother's shoulders. "My dad's death has turned everything upside down. Mom's leaving the day after tomorrow for an extended visit with my eldest brother, Garrett. While she's gone, I'll be taking over the day-to-day responsibilities on the Circle P."

"And you're…letting me go?" Emma's stomach punched the down button on the express elevator to the basement. True, she hadn't signed a contract, not yet, but

Seth had sent a check to cover her travel expenses and promised to reimburse the cost of shipping the rest of her meager possessions. She turned toward her daughter. How would she explain the sudden change in plans to Bree? Her child had been nearly as excited about horses and cowboys as Emma had been for the opportunity to work on the ranch that was rapidly making a name for itself as a vacation destination.

Doris's eyes widened. "Oh, no," she said hurriedly. "That's not what I meant. Not at all." She cleared her throat. "I know it's a lot to ask, but I was wondering if you'd take over the kitchen right away. We'd all be grateful if you would."

Stunned, Emma rocked back on her heels. She pictured herself standing at the sink where bright sunshine flooded through windows dressed in cheery prints. She imagined the dishes she'd create on the massive cookstove, the salads and cold soups she'd chill in the built-in refrigerators. Behind a door at the end of the kitchen stood a pantry any chef would give their eyeteeth to control. How could she say no?

She straightened. "Ms. Judd, I'm honored that you think so highly of me, but aren't you rushing things a bit?" She cast a look at Colt's sullen expression. No doubt about it—the man did not want her here.

Her gaze swung to the widow whose grief was so new and raw. She ached to help Doris. But, for more reasons than she could count, working for Colt was a bad idea. Despite his striking good looks, from the moment he'd practically collided with her on the front porch, he hadn't cared whose feelings he trampled.

"I was in here earlier. Believe me, it didn't look like

this." Doris gestured toward the spotless kitchen. "It seems as if you already have everything well in hand."

Emma hesitated. Warming up a few casseroles the neighbors had dropped off, that was one thing. Preparing meals for an army of hungry cowboys, that was something else again. She'd counted on learning the ins and outs of catering to paying guests and ranch hands alike from the woman who had held the job for a lifetime.

Colt stepped into the breach. "Let me make one thing perfectly clear. Don't think you're going to change things around here. Tradition is very important on the Circle P. We like everything just the way it is."

Emma let her voice drop into its coolest register. "Exactly how am I supposed to follow the routine when I don't even know what it is?"

"Now, don't you worry about that," Doris said soothingly. "Someone with your training and experience can probably cook rings around me." She crossed to a cabinet, where she withdrew a notebook so worn it was held together by rubber bands. Almost reverently, she held it out to Emma. "This has been handed down by generations of cooks on the Circle P. It holds all the recipes our guests and employees have come to associate with the ranch. Use it, and you'll do fine. Why don't you take a good look at it tonight. We can go over any questions you might have tomorrow."

Emma traced her fingers over the worn leather cover. Every restaurant had its tried-and-true recipes. Most chefs guarded them religiously, never letting the secrets to their success out of their sight. She'd even heard rumors of cooks who slept with their recipe collections under their pillows. And yet, Doris had entrusted such a treasure to her?

"I'll take very good care of it," she promised. She tucked a loose slip of paper deeper into the book.

"I think we should have a trial period," Colt broke in. "Three months to see if she's up to the job or not."

From the way he glared at her, Emma suspected the new boss would mark off every one of the next ninety days on the calendar, counting the hours until he got rid of her.

Doris peered up at her son. "I'm not sure I'll be back that soon. Garrett's baby is due in October. I'll want to stay with them for a while afterward. Let's say another month or more." She turned pleading eyes on Emma. "Please say you'll stay that long. I'm sure this will be a permanent position."

Emma blinked, thinking of the plusses that had drawn her to accept the job—the relaxed atmosphere that was so different from Chef Larue's nightly screaming matches, the excellent public schools nearby, free room and board and a chance to put down roots. Even if things didn't work out on the Circle P, in a few months she'd build a solid nest egg. One that would see her and Bree through while she found another position.

She pressed the cookbook to her chest. "I'll read through this tonight, as soon as Bree and I get settled in."

"Oh!" Doris's eyes filled with fresh tears. "We were supposed to clean out the little house for you. With all that's gone on this week, the thought never crossed my mind."

"Don't worry, Mom." Though Colt's protective arm around his mom's shoulders tightened, he sent Emma another dark look. "I'll put Royce and Randy on it first thing in the morning. They'll have it all sorted out by nightfall. In the meantime, she can stay in my room."

No way. No how.

Emma's whole body stiffened. Though Colt was handsome enough to make her back teeth ache, if sleeping with the boss was part of the deal, she'd take Bree and head for her car this minute.

At her sharp inhale, a smug expression crept over Colt's face. "No need to get your dander up. I'll bunk in with Garrett."

Doris slipped the end of a messy braid over one shoulder. "If ya'll don't mind, I think I'd like to lie down for a while, after all."

Emma waited until the tall cowboy steered his mother out the door before she drew in a thready breath. So far, nothing about her move to Florida had gone according to plan. She'd come to the Circle P in the hopes of one day running her own kitchen, not having the job thrust upon her the moment she set foot on the ranch. She'd counted on learning whatever she needed to know about trail rides and hoedowns under Doris's calm tutelage. She certainly hadn't planned on working with Colt, but she wouldn't let him keep her from doing her job. She ran her fingers down the front of her jacket, straightening the crisp white fabric.

"Come on, Bree," she said, holding out her hand. "Let's unload the car and find out where we're staying tonight."

LEATHER CREAKED AS Colt flipped the stirrup over Star's back. He tapped the gelding's middle and waited for the horse to expel air before he cinched the front girth strap.

"I miss this." Garrett's voice drifted over the partition between the stalls. "Ridin' out at first light. The smell of hay and horseflesh. The quiet. You don't get this in Atlanta. Too many cars. Too many people."

Colt grabbed the back strap and threaded it through the buckle. "Bet you don't miss the skeeters and the snakes. Mucking out stalls." He gave the saddle a final tug. Satisfied it was secure, he lowered the stirrup into place.

"You get up on the wrong side of the bed?"

"Not my bed," Colt grunted. "Besides, you snore."

He lifted a sweat-stained Stetson from a nearby nail, ran a hand through his hair and plopped the hat on his head. The kitchen had been dark and vacant when he'd passed through on his way to the barn. He'd thought about rapping on his bedroom door, rousting the new cook and telling her she was already running late. But he'd lingered in the house only long enough to spoon grounds and pour water into a battered coffeemaker. He'd promised his mom he'd give Emma a chance. If nothing else, he was a man of his word.

Besides, the woman wouldn't last. Certainly not six months. Heck, he bet she wouldn't stick around long enough for the next cattle drive. Her slim frame wasn't made for the heavy workload that came with life on a ranch. The hours she kept were better suited to the big city.

Not that he had checked up on her or anything.

It was only happenstance that he'd noticed how late she'd stayed up last night. It took an entire crew of men, working long days in the blazing heat or the pouring rain, to keep the Circle P in the black. He needed to know the status of every task, every chore, each of the ranch's thousand head of cattle before Ty and Sarah took off on their vacation. So, after dinner, he and Ty had locked themselves in the office. Midnight had come and gone before they finished. Passing by his old room on his way to Garrett's, he'd spotted a spill of light seeping under the door and wondered if he should check on their guest.

Had she settled in? Was the bed comfortable? Did she want him to join her in it?

Yeah, like that was gonna happen.

Considering the particular shade of red Emma had turned when he'd offered her his room, she'd more likely slap his face than invite him in. Which was fine by him. Though he wouldn't pretend he hadn't noticed the soft curves under her jeans and jacket. She had the kind of wholesome good looks that started a guy thinking of white picket fences. But he had no room in his life for that. Or a kid. Even a cute one like Bree. Not when he spent nine months out of the year traveling from one rodeo venue to another.

Clucking to the big gelding, Colt stepped into the wide aisle between the rows of stalls. Metal jangled as Star tossed his head.

"Easy, boy." He ran a hand down the horse's neck.

"Where are we headed today?" Garrett led a brown mare out of a stall.

Thankful for the chance to get his thoughts back on track, Colt resettled his hat. "Thought we'd follow the fence line along Ol' Man Tompkins's property. The boys patched one hole. There's probably others. We need to be on the lookout for his Brahmans, too. They've been making a habit of crossing onto the Circle P."

"Good work for a mornin'."

In the stillness of the predawn light, horseshoes rang against cedar floorboards that had survived a hundred years, and would probably be around for another century. Leading Star into the yard, Colt sniffed the still air and frowned when he didn't smell bacon. "I need coffee before we head out. You?"

"Now you're talkin'. Pregnant women and caffeine don't mix. I've been sneakin' off to Starbucks ever since the stick turned blue," Garrett said as they crossed the yard to a hitching post just off the back patio.

"It'll be worth it when you hold that baby the first time." Colt clapped a hand on his big brother's shoulder. "I can't believe you had it in you, bro."

"Yeah, well. We have a long way to go yet."

Colt hiked an eyebrow at the odd remark, but he was too busy surveying the darkened kitchen to give Garrett's problems much more than a passing thought. Overhead fluorescents buzzed and lit the room when he flipped the switch by the door. The red light on the coffeepot was the only sign of life.

Garrett clapped his hands together. "Looks like we're on our own this morning."

While Colt filled a couple of to-go cups and a thermos, his brother pried the lid off a plastic container he found on the counter. "There's plenty of pound cake. Want a hunk or two?"

Colt rubbed his stomach. What he really wanted was bacon and eggs. Some of his mom's biscuits. A side of grits. He shook his head. He might have promised to give the new cook a chance, but it wouldn't be long before the rest of the crew wandered into the house expecting a hearty meal. What would happen then?

Garrett must have sensed his glum mood because he said, "Mom'll talk to Emma. Make sure she understands we jump on the day a bit earlier than she's used to."

Colt stifled a sigh. "I'll let her slide for today. But mark my words, this'll be the last time. Can't expect the men to do a full day's work on empty bellies."

He hefted the mugs and headed for the door, his boots leaving dusty prints across the floor. "Let's ride. I want to be back before the vet gets here this afternoon." According to Ty, one of their bulls had tangled with barbed wire last week and was acting peculiar. He'd left word with the ranch hands to bring the animal into one of the pens by the barn.

Two hours later, the fence posts checked and a repair to one section noted, Colt sloshed the dregs of cold coffee onto a nearby palmetto bush. A pair of osprey had built their nest in the bleached skeleton of a tree on the Tompkins property. He shaded his eyes, watching as one of the adults dropped a fish to its young. The sounds of the juveniles feeding reminded him that he needed to stop by the kitchen when they got back to make sure the rest of the crew had been fed.

He tugged on Star's reins, slowing the horse. Garrett pulled up alongside.

"What do we know about this new cook?" Colt asked, pouring fresh coffee from the thermos.

Garrett shrugged. "You know as much as I do. Mom and Dad ate at the restaurant she worked in. They liked her enough to hire her, I guess."

"That's another thing." Colt frowned over coffee too cold to drink. "Did you know about that trip? I haven't been in touch as often as I should have, but still…you'd think I would have known."

The osprey took flight, wings flapping as it headed south for another fish. His eyes tracking the bird, Garrett stared into the distance. "They didn't mention it to me, but then, I've been a little preoccupied with Arlene."

Colt shifted in his saddle. "Much as I'm glad Mom's going to stay with you for a bit, I hope she changes her mind and comes back to the Circle P soon."

"Because of one missed breakfast?" Garrett's head swiveled toward him.

"Nah, it's more than that." He dashed the last of his drink on the ground. "That Emma, she's too pretty. Next thing you know, the ranch hands'll be spending all their free time in the kitchen."

"Pretty, huh?"

Colt clamped his lips shut. One more word and he'd be the subject of all too much ribbing from the rest of the Judds. There was no denying the petite brunette had gotten under his skin, but more than her good looks bothered him.

He turned aside, keeping his hands busy tying his mug to his saddle. "We do things different here. That's all I'm sayin'."

"Whatever happens, I hope you're wrong. Arlene and me, we really need Mom right now."

At his brother's tone, the hairs at the back of Colt's neck stood to attention. He canted his head to get a better look at Garrett's face, but his brother had pulled his hat low over his eyes. "What's up?" he asked.

Garrett took a breath so deep his shoulders shuddered. "I didn't want to get everybody stirred up yesterday. We'd just come back from buryin' Dad, and the last thing Mom needed was more bad news. But Arlene's got preeclampsia. They're having the devil's own time getting her blood pressure under control. Doc says if she carries the baby to term—and that's a big *if*—she could have a stroke. Or worse." His head drooped.

Colt's chest tightened. What he knew about women and babies wouldn't fill a feed bucket, but he'd seen cows go down with eclampsia. If a rancher knew about it in time, he called the vet. Even then, everybody had to step mighty lively or they lost both the cow and the calf. His face warmed. Here he'd been bellyaching about skipping a meal when his own brother faced the prospect of losing his wife and unborn child. He pulled himself straighter in his saddle.

Whatever it took, he vowed, he'd do his part to make sure his mom could stay with Garrett and Arlene for as long as she was needed.

Even if it meant putting up with a few hunger pangs.

From somewhere nearby, a throaty engine roared to life. Emma slung an arm over her head, but quickly realized she could have saved herself the effort. With no curtains to block it, sunlight seeped beneath her eyelids, invaded her sleep and chased away the image of a dark-haired man whose lips had been created for kissing.

Not that she wanted another man in her life. Or her dreams for that matter. Not at all.

She pried her lids open. Her vision filled with the soft buttery hues of gold and warm cinnamon. Momentarily disoriented, she focused on the smoothly finished wood ceiling, letting awareness of her surroundings gradually seep in, the way she'd done all too often during a root-less childhood.

She was at the Circle P. In Colt's room. In Colt's bed.

"Hey, lazybones," she whispered, skimming a hand

over the clean sheets she'd spread across the mattress before putting Bree down for the night.

She smiled, pleased at the way Ty and Sarah's son Jimmy had taken her daughter under his wing. Despite their age difference, the two had played together long past Bree's usual bedtime. So long, in fact, that her little girl had fallen asleep before she'd finished her evening snack.

Now, if only *she'd* been able to drift off as quickly, Emma thought.

Truth be told, the fresh linens had done nothing to mask a distinctly masculine scent. It had tickled her nose, stirring an awareness of Colt that had kept her awake far too late after a day behind the wheel and her poorly timed arrival at the ranch. Unable to sleep, she'd sat up half the night, skimming through the Circle P's cookbook, identifying favorite dishes by their dog-eared pages, by the number of stains and food splotches.

Small wonder, then, that she and Bree had both slept in.

Her fingers reached the end of the mattress without discovering her little girl's warm, familiar shape. Emma scrambled from the bed.

"Bree?" She scanned the thin blankets. No child-shaped lump hid beneath them.

A hollow spot opened in the pit of her stomach. According to Bree, monsters lived under the bed. Doubting her daughter would hide under one, Emma peered beneath theirs just the same. A light coating of dust and nothing more covered the glossy hardwood. She crossed to the closet and flung open the bifold door. A fresh wave of Colt's scent wafted out at her. She held her breath and poked through clothes on hangers, boots and a pair of men's black dress shoes.

No Bree.

Her heart thudding, Emma thrust her legs into the jeans she'd discarded on a chair. She pulled yesterday's T-shirt over her pajamas and shoved her arms into the sleeves. Her bare feet skimming over polished wood, she padded down the hall.

"Bree," she called, pausing to look over the railing into the great room. Her gaze swept past inviting leather couches, a scattering of chairs and recliners. Pillows lined the hearth, but Bree hadn't curled up on one. Her dark curls weren't bent over Mrs. Wickles in the rocking chair.

Where is she?

Emma raced down the stairs, crossed the great room on a dead run and headed for the kitchen. She skidded into the room, fear lodged in her throat. Spotting a head full of dark curls at the huge trestle table, she drank in a breath of pure relief. She let it out slowly, noting the empty grape stem and slice of toast on a plate.

"Mommy, I saw cowboys. Lots of them. They came in for breakfast." A milk mustache moved up and down above Bree's lips. "Mr. Colt and Mr.— What was his name?" She looked across the table at Doris.

"Garrett, honey," Doris answered. Dressed in jeans and a shirt with Western piping, she looked as at home on the ranch as the cowboys Bree referred to.

Bree's head bobbed up and down. "Mr. Garrett. They got on horses and went for a ride. Mr. Garrett and Mr. Colt are brothers. Did you know that, Mommy? Jimmy has brothers, too. Tim and Chris. Why don't I have a brother?" She stopped for a breath.

"Briana Elizabeth Shane, you scared me half to death," Emma whispered. "You weren't supposed to leave the room without me."

Her face all wide-eyed innocence, Bree protested, "But there were cowboys, Mommy!"

A smile flitted across Doris's lips. "Hard to argue with the child's logic. Coffee?" She lifted a cup.

"I'll get it." Padding past nearly empty pans of sweet rolls and coffee cakes on the counter, Emma frowned. A slice of melon and a couple of strawberries rested in the bottom of an immense bowl. She nibbled on her lower lip.

"Looks like the cavalry came through. Do they usually get started this early?" She stifled a yawn. The restaurants where she'd worked in the past had opened late, and closed in the wee hours of the morning, another reason why the move to Florida had been a good one. But just how early did the day start on the ranch?

Doris waved a hand, dismissive. "I probably shoulda mentioned that. Since I was already up, I threw enough together to keep the boys from starvin' to death."

"You couldn't sleep?"

"Can't get used to the quiet, I guess." Doris stretched. "Seth snored like a band saw." She blotted her eyes.

Emma held her breath, wanting to give the new widow a chance to talk about her husband, but not quite sure what to say about the man she'd barely known. When Doris busied herself brushing a few crumbs from the table, she took it as a sign to pick up the thread of their earlier conversation.

"What time do you usually put breakfast on the table?"

Doris shrugged. "Depends. In the summer, we get an

early start because of the heat. A little later in winter. Either way, before the roosters crow. Somewhere between six and seven. There's a bell out on the patio. I ring it when the food's ready, and they hustle in."

Six? Her internal clock was going to need a serious adjustment.

"I'm sorry," she said, grabbing a mug. "I won't let it happen again." She tugged her hair out from underneath the back of her T-shirt.

"Where is everyone?" she asked. Though they were alone in the room, the last thing she needed was for Colt to walk through the door and accuse her of slacking off.

"Oh, they're all busy. Garrett and Colt are checking the fence lines between us and Ol' Man Tompkins's place." Doris hefted her coffee mug to the west. "Always a problem there." She took a sip. "Randy and Royce took Tim and Chris with 'em to work on the little house. Ty and Sarah dropped Jimmy off to play with his friend at the Gillmores'. I think Sarah's upstairs packing. Ty's wrapping up things in the office. The others are out doing whatever they have to do to keep body and soul together."

It sounded as if everyone had a job and, except for her, they were hard at work doing it. Emma tugged her jeans a bit higher on her hips and wished she'd thought to put on a belt. "What can I do to help out?"

"Nothin' right now. Supper's taken care of. Stacy Gillmore sent Ty and Sarah back with enough beef stew to feed an army. There's still plenty of rolls and salads left over from yesterday."

A shadow passed over Doris's face. She pinched the edge from one of the coffee cakes, and placed it on her plate but didn't eat it. Before Emma could ask if she was all right, the older woman found her bearings and continued. "The men eat sandwiches for lunch—I usually pack them the night before so's all they have to do is grab 'em and go. Peanut butter and jelly, mostly. You never know where they'll be working. Might not have access to a fridge."

Emma nodded. Bagged lunches sounded easy enough and put her concerns about the lunch service to rest. She crossed from the cupboard to the coffeepot and poured herself a cup. "Sounds like we have a few things to go over," she suggested. She cautioned herself to proceed slowly. For weeks after Jack's funeral, she'd drifted through life in a fog. Just because Doris had rolled out of bed at her usual time and skipped the widow's weeds, that didn't mean she was operating at full steam.

"I have a few things left to stash in my suitcase." Doris drained the last of her cup. "Let me do that, and we can get started."

"Great. We'll get washed up—" Emma nodded toward Bree's milky mouth "—and be right back down." She topped off her mug and held out a hand to her daughter. "Come on, sweetie. Let's go get dressed."

The little girl scrambled down from her chair. "Will we see horses today, Mommy? Can I ride one?"

The thought of her child sitting astride a big horse was enough to send concern shivering down Emma's spine.

"On a ranch like the Circle P, everybody has to be able to handle a horse," Doris said quietly. "It's practically in the job description."

Maybe, but Emma waved a hand toward a sink full of dirty dishes. "For now, I think I'd better concentrate on all this."

Minutes later, while she brushed the sleep tangles

from Bree's hair, Emma used the time to impress on her four-year-old the importance of following the rules.

"Remember how, in the city, you weren't allowed to cross the street without holding my hand?"

Bree nodded solemnly. "Always watch for the blinking man. He'll tell you when it's safe. Look both ways. And hold Mommy's hand or the cars will knock me down." She tipped her head up at Emma. "But, Mommy, there aren't any cars here. Just cowboys."

"On a ranch, we have different things to watch out for. Horses weigh a lot. If one of them stepped on your foot, it'd hurt. Cows—you saw those sharp horns. A little girl like you could get poked." She prodded Bree's ribs and listened to her daughter laugh. She took a breath. "So never wander off on your own."

Making a rule for her four-year-old was one thing. Trusting her daughter to obey it was something else. While she brushed her own hair into a no-nonsense ponytail, Emma wondered if she'd done the right thing by moving them to a place where she hardly knew what was safe for herself, much less for her child.

She blinked slowly. New York had a lot to offer, but she'd been hemmed in by tall buildings, crowds and traffic. In a city known for its five-star restaurants, the chance to run her own kitchen had been at least ten years in her future. Worse, her twelve- and fourteen-hour days began at noon and stretched into the wee hours of the morning. Which meant, other than on her days off, she rarely caught more than a glimpse of her daughter.

Was that the kind of future she wanted?

Here, she'd barely stepped on the premises before she'd been handed the chance to be her own boss. True, the hours were long, and she still hadn't seen the little house they kept saying would be hers and Bree's, but even in the middle of a funeral, everyone had gone out of their way to give her and her daughter a warm welcome.

She stared out the immense picture window overlooking the front yard. Beyond the barn, flat land stretched for more miles than she could cover in a day's walk. There were trees for Bree to climb, grassy lawns to play on and room for an active four-year-old to romp.

The only fly in the ointment was Colt. The altercation with the tall rancher still rankled. She was certain their problems were far from over. And, once Doris and the Parkers left, there'd be no one to run interference for her with the handsome man who oh so obviously didn't want her on his ranch.

Chapter Three

Sunlight filtered through the kitchen's screened door. Declaring the oasis the perfect spot, Bree dumped an armload of doll clothes in the puddle of sunshine.

"Mrs. Wickles and me are gonna watch for cowboys." She pressed her nose against the wire mesh. "I want them to come to my tea party."

"Stay inside." Emma placed her own supplies on the kitchen table. "Ms. Doris said everybody went to work early this morning. They won't be back again till dinner."

Though she doubted Bree would wander off—not so soon after their talk—Emma reached past her daughter to hook the latch. Beyond the patio, an old dog lounged in the shade beneath the oak tree. A black bird larger than any crow she'd ever seen pecked at the grass. A distant pond glistened, and she wondered if it held fish. Fresh-caught and grilled to perfection, almost any kind of seafood made a nice meal. She crossed to the table, where she added a note to a list she'd started while looking through the Circle P's treasured cookbook the night before.

Mission accomplished, she tugged on the hem of the simple floral blouse she'd chosen instead of her chef's whites. With Bree playing quietly, Emma plunged a sticky pan into an immense copper sink that made her fears of rusty appliances and warped counters seem silly. There were changes to make, of course. Storing dishes in the cabinet opposite the fridge meant having to cross the kitchen every time she reached for a glass. The battered thirty-cup percolator was older than she was. It would have to go. The bread box sat too close to the stove. But, all in all, things were in far better shape than she'd expected.

She finished washing the pan and set it aside to drain. Deciding the best way to preserve her job was to avoid another run-in with Colt, she vowed to keep her distance from the imposing cowboy. Besides, she had other, more pressing, problems. Last night, she'd scratched her head over the oldest recipes in the Circle P's cookbook. Some of them were little more than a list of ingredients. She supposed niceties like temperatures and cooking times had been handed down from one generation to another. While she loved the idea of being part of that tradition, those other cooks had worked together for years. She needed to learn all they'd absorbed in just one day.

One day. How was she ever going to do it?

When Doris returned just as she was drying the last of the dishes, Emma opened her laptop and found her notes.

"Okay, so biscuits." Her fingers poised over the keyboard. "From all accounts, they're your specialty. Several former guests even mentioned them on the website." She squeezed her eyes closed and swallowed. "I have to admit, that's something I've never quite mastered."

Doris sipped from an ever-present cup of coffee. "The secret to a good biscuit is a light touch. I mix up all the dry ingredients and keep them over there." She motioned toward a large ceramic bowl on the dry sink. "There's oil in the cupboard overhead. Add it and the milk at the same time. Don't stir any more than you have to. Pat out the dough. Don't roll it."

Emma typed furiously, stopping only when Doris pushed her coffee aside and stood.

"Or you can do what I've done the past ten years." She crossed to the big Sub-Zero and pulled open the lowest storage bin. "You can use these." She held up a popular brand of canned biscuits.

Stunned, Emma sat back in her chair. "You're kidding, right?"

Doris pointed to an age-lined face. "Do I look like I'm joking?"

Emma searched the woman's blue eyes for a hint of humor and found none.

"But—" she protested. "But what about the traditions Colt said were so important?"

"Honey, Colt's just like you—brand-new to the job and eager to make an impression. My advice? Don't waste time on the small stuff. I've been serving store-bought at the house for the better part of a decade, and nobody's been the wiser." She gazed through the window over the sink. "I'd do it on the trail rides, but the cans are a mite harder to hide out there."

Emma blew out a long, slow breath. Learning the older cook had a few ready-made tricks up her sleeves took some of the stress off her shoulders. Her confidence bolstered, she returned to the task at hand.

"Okay," she said, "what's next?"

For hours, they pored over the cookbook while Bree chatted with Mrs. Wickles and played with her dolls.

"I'll never get all this right," Emma mused when they finally took a break.

Menus at the Circle P were at once simple and challenging. According to Doris, oven-fried chicken and mashed potatoes were nearly as popular as swamp cabbage, a dish Emma had never heard of, much less prepared. Apparently, it involved harvesting the hearts from palm trees.

How was she supposed to do that, she wondered.

"You're gonna make mistakes. Everybody does," Doris soothed. "The first time I fixed meat loaf, I was so proud of it. When I took it out of the oven, the bacon and tomato crust on top was perfect. The edges, dark and crispy. Seth said it was so pretty, it set his mouth watering. That was before I sliced into it."

She slapped the table, tears and laughter sparkling in her eyes. "It literally poured out of the pan. Seth ladled it over his mashed potatoes and said it was the best gravy he'd ever tasted."

Her laughter faded and she wiped her eyes with the edge of her apron. "I'm sure gonna miss that old man."

"I'm not sure Colt would think a ruined meal was something to laugh at," Emma mumbled. For the life of her, she couldn't picture the big man smiling about… anything.

"My boys—they all have their moments—but I couldn't ask for better sons." Doris slanted her head to the side. "You can tell a lot about a man by the way he treats his mother. Take my Seth, for example." The older woman's face crinkled. "Oh, that man. I was a sales clerk at the five-and-dime in town when he came in to buy a birthday present. For his mother, as it turned out."

Emma smiled at Doris's meaningful glance.

"One look at him, and I just knew I'd found the one I'd spend the rest of my life with." She sipped her coffee. "You'll see. It'll happen for you, too."

Emma shook her head. The kind of love Doris and Seth had shared sounded like something straight out of a fairy tale. She doubted whether a modern-day Prince Charming existed. Certainly not one for her. Colt, with his piercing blue eyes and all that gorgeous thick black hair might look the part, but true heroes didn't have his temper.

And wasn't she done with angry men?

From her dad to Jack, she'd had enough. As for the chefs in the kitchens where she'd worked, if she'd had any idea how much they threw their weight around, she'd have chosen another line of work entirely.

Here on the Circle P, things would be different. The ranch hands, from the little she'd seen of them, stuck to themselves or had families of their own. Soon, all the Judd brothers except Colt would leave. He'd only be here until his younger brothers took over. Knowing the man was another in a line of Mr. Wrongs, she'd keep her distance. Something that should be easy enough to do as long as she put dinner on the table at six and provided a hearty breakfast for the ranchers before their day started.

"So," Doris asked at last, "do you think you're up to the job? I hate to dump all this on you the minute you show up. But it sounds as if Garrett and Arlene could use my help." She wiped her eyes. "It'll be good for me to get away for a while."

Emma's eyes swept the immaculate kitchen. She drummed her fingers on the cookbook.

"Yes," she answered with far more certainty than she'd felt at the start of the day.

Alone with Bree a short time later, Emma flipped through recipes until she came to a cobbler that, according to her notes, was one of Doris's favorites. It sounded like just the thing to prepare as a thank-you gift. She ducked into the pantry. As she searched the shelves for key ingredients, she tilted her head at an odd noise.

"Bree, is someone knocking at the door?" she called.

In the breathless pause before her daughter answered, Emma considered stepping into the kitchen for a look.

"No, Mommy. No one's here," Bree said at last.

Emma twisted a can to read the label. "Are you playing?"

"I'm looking outside."

"Try not to jiggle the door, honey." She pictured the four-year-old, her nose pressed against the screen, the door rattling against the latch. Adding jars of sliced apples to her pile, she gathered the items for the cobbler in her arms. Before she'd taken two steps into the kitchen, Emma froze. Sunshine poured in through the screened door, illuminating the vacant space where, minutes earlier, she'd left her daughter.

Her heart in her throat for the second time that day, Emma gasped.

"Bree!"

"You sure you know how to fix it?" Colt leaned over his saddle horn to give his brother a doubtful look. The air-conditioning unit in the little house had spewed nothing but dust when Randy and Royce tested it this morning. It was broken, they'd insisted. It needed to be replaced.

Colt slapped one hand against his jeans. A big bill would not get his stint as manager off to a good start. Especially since he was already going to owe the vet for a house call.

"While you were busy earning a gold buckle on the rodeo circuit, I was fixing air conditioners part-time to

pay my way through college. Remember?" Palmetto
rustled as Garrett guided his mare off the main trail,
headed for the house that had been sitting vacant for the
better part of two years.

"Just don't spend any more money than necessary,"
Colt cautioned. He was all for making the place habit-
able. No more, no less. Not for a cook who probably
wouldn't stay on the ranch through the heat of summer.

His stomach rumbled, a reminder that he'd missed
breakfast. That *she'd* missed breakfast. He tipped his
hat back to swipe his forehead with a damp sleeve and
caught a glimpse of the sun on the wrong side of noon.
His first day on the job, and he was already falling behind. Temporary repairs to the fence the Circle P shared
with Ol' Man Tompkins had taken longer than he wanted
to spend on them. A permanent fix was in order and,
with Garrett tied up at the little house, it was looking
more and more like he'd have to take care of it himself.

Tack jangled and leather creaked as he urged Star
into a trot that would take them home for more supplies.
Nearing the barn, he reined the horse to a walk when he
spied one of the ranch hands lounging in the shade. His
nose in a book, the boy gave every indication that there
was nothing better to do on the busy ranch than stand
there all day chewing on a piece of straw. Colt urged Star
toward the young man who, according to Ty, tended to
slack off whenever he could.

"Josh, I need you to grab a couple of posts and some
wire. Head on over to the spot where the creek runs
between our land and Tompkins's. There's two places
where his cows have broken through our fence again."

Josh barely looked up from his reading material. He
shifted a strand of hay from one side of his mouth to

the other. "Sure thing, Colt. I'll get to it soon as I'm finished here."

Colt blinked slowly. "That's *boss* to you." Recalling how his dad had dealt with ornery ranch hands, he let his vowels stretch out, emphasizing his drawl to show he meant business. "I think that barn can stand on its own without your help. Unless you want to spend all night roundin' up strays, you'd best get a move on."

Thpt. A tiny divot appeared in the gray sand at Josh's feet.

"I'm helpin' the vet right now."

Excuse me? He'd expected the older hands on the ranch to test him. Not a young kid like Josh.

Behind his sunglasses, Colt's vision narrowed in on Jim Jacobs's truck parked near the holding pen.

"That the vet?" His voice deceptively mild, he inclined his head toward the man who sat in the front seat, his phone pressed against one ear.

"Yep. That's him."

"Seems to me, he doesn't need your help this minute." Squaring his shoulders, Colt pulled himself erect atop Star. Clearly, it was going to take a firmer hand than he'd expected to keep things on an even keel on the Circle P. "Now, I've told you what needs to be done. The choice is up to you. Get movin' or start packin'." He glared at the young man, daring him to argue.

Josh faced him for a long second before he shoved his book into a back pocket. He started toward the shed where they stored fencing materials. Watching him go, Colt let out a slow whistle. He patted Star's long neck and wished everyone who worked on the ranch was as easy to handle as his horse.

"Come on, boy." He gave the reins a tug. "Let's go say hello."

The man who stepped from the vet's truck a few minutes later had put on thirty pounds and lost his swagger, but Colt easily recognized the former rodeo competitor. After their first season on the circuit together, Jim Jacobs had chosen vet school over bronco bustin' and calf tying. Now he peered up from beneath a baseball cap, sorrow showing on a face that had aged since they'd last seen each other.

"Sorry I wasn't able to make it to the funeral. I got stuck at the Carson place. That big bay of theirs ran through an electric fence and got himself all cut up. What a mess."

"We had a good turnout." Colt concentrated on combing his free hand through Star's mane. He'd been in such a fog during the service and the gathering at the house afterward, he wasn't sure who'd shown up and who hadn't.

Jim stood with his hands on his hips. "Everybody around here's gonna miss Seth. I heard one of you boys was gonna take his place. Who drew the short straw?"

"News travels fast." The privilege of running the Circle P was one he had asked for. Colt grimaced, his gut tightening. "It's gonna be tough, but I'll manage." He added an aw-shucks grin to let his old friend know he was up to the job.

Jim mulled over the news and then, with a grunt and a nod, he grabbed his bag from the front seat. "You've been around horses and cattle all your life. You'll do just fine." He crossed to the holding pen where an enormous bull stood, docilely chewing his cud. "Now, let's see about this bad boy."

Colt eyed a bright gash in the animal's glossy brown coat. After ten years riding some of the meanest bulls on the rodeo circuit, he knew a thing or two about them. Some had dispositions as gentle as the one in the picture book that had been his favorite when he was Bree's age. Others could be sweet as clover one second and madder than a wet cat the next. Whatever their mood, two thousand pounds of muscle and horns earned the animals a healthy dose of respect. But livestock weren't pets. They didn't have names. As the third of four bulls on the ranch, this one was simply referred to by number.

"Three tangled with some downed wire a week or so ago. It's probably infected."

"Anything else I should know?" Jim reached for the latch.

"I don't know much more than that," Colt admitted. With a start, he realized Josh had probably been tasked to provide more details on the animal's history. "You need someone on the gate?"

"Nah, I got this," Jim said.

Only, he didn't. Instead of raising his head the way he should have, Three didn't so much as twitch when Jim slid back the latch. The animal didn't even look at the man entering his pen. In fact, a low, rumbling *mmrruuh* was Three's only indication that he was paying attention at all.

"Uh, Jim…" Colt reached for his rope.

The warning came too late. No sooner did the vet ease the gate wide enough to step through than Three charged across the pen.

Jim yelped and jumped to one side. Stumbling out of the bull's path, he lost his grip on the metal bar. The gate swung wide.

Three exploded out of the pen and into the yard.

"Aw, crap," Colt muttered. Out of the corner of one eye, he saw Jim scramble over the fence and *into* the pen. Though he was probably safer there than out in the yard, that still left the not-so-little matter of a loose bull for somebody to deal with. The animal stood in the center of the space between the barn and the greenhouse.

"No harm. No foul."

Slowly, Colt walked Star toward the beast.

Think again, he told himself a second later when Bree Shane peeked around the corner of the house. The girl gave a quick wave before ducking out of sight.

Colt's chest seized. "Stay away. Stay away," he whispered.

Moments later, Bree raced around the corner. This time, she didn't stop, but headed straight into the yard, pigtails flying. Colt's mouth filled with sawdust.

The motion drew Three's attention. His head lowered, he pawed the ground.

Colt swore. His heart rate kicked into a gallop.

"Get back," he yelled, not caring whether the bull or the child obeyed as long as one of them did.

Bree skidded to stop. "Mr. Colt," she called. "Can I pet the cow?"

"No!" His eyes on a bull that could charge with devastating results, Colt spurred Star into action. Dirt sprayed from the gelding's hooves as he positioned the horse between the girl and certain death.

"Get back in the house!"

Bree didn't move. Star's hooves pranced over the dirt, throwing up clods.

"Get inside. Right now!"

The kid's mouth dropped wide open. More sound than

Colt ever thought possible spewed out. The high, shrill voice startled the bull. Three shook his head, turned and trotted toward the greenhouse.

Watching a ton of hooved, horned danger hustle to escape the noise, Colt spared a look behind him. The slap of the kitchen door told him Bree had scampered to safety. Relief uncoiled through his chest and he sucked in air. He unfurled his rope and worked it into a lasso. Step by step, he advanced on Three, flung the business end of a lariat over the bull's massive horns and led him toward the pen.

While Jim clambered over the fence again, Colt dismounted and gave Star a well-deserved pat. Trying to make light of the situation, he grinned and nudged the vet.

"This time, don't let him out."

But there was nothing lighthearted about the way his stomach dipped when Colt considered what might have happened if he and Star hadn't been there.

"I'll send someone out to help as soon as I can," he told Jim. "First, though, there's a little kid who needs to know the importance of doing what she's told."

Intending to read both Bree and her mom the riot act, he headed for the house. Ty Parker met him halfway there. The owner hiked a thumb over one shoulder at the kitchen he'd just exited.

"I wouldn't go inside if I was you. Crying kids. Angry women. General confusion." Ty doffed his hat. "Want to tell me what happened?"

Colt squared his shoulders. "My fault." He refused to dodge the blame. As manager, anything that happened on the Circle P was his responsibility. "I didn't realize Three was an escape artist. I should have known bet-

ter. Should have let Josh help the vet like he was supposed to."

"Anyone hurt?" Ty wanted to know.

"Just my pride." Colt clenched and unclenched a fist.
"We were lucky." He eyed the door at the end of the path.
"You want to tell 'em for me?"

"Nah, man. I'm smarter than that." Ty's feet were already in motion. "I'll help Jim with the bull."

Colt didn't doubt for a minute he'd drawn the tougher
job. One look through the kitchen door only reinforced
his certainty that if he had anything better to do, he'd
choose it rather than face the crowd clustered around
Bree.

He eased into the room. Knowing he'd have to wait
for the excitement to fade, Colt grabbed a glass from the
cupboard and poured himself a tall iced tea. He drank
it down in one long gulp while he tried to steady his
hands. He closed his eyes, but the image of massive
horns tossing a tiny body into the air played against the
backs of his lids. He groaned, thinking of all the times
he'd been thrown from a bucking bull's back. Landing
always hurt. And there'd been that time in Laredo when
Ol' Hickory got his head under him and sent him flying.
Nothing about that night had gone well.

Behind him, Bree's sobs gradually quieted down
enough that a man could make himself heard. He pushed
away from the counter. Tea sloshed in his empty stomach as he spun to face the room.

Still clutching her daughter to her chest, Emma turned
a tear-stained face in his direction. Her hair had spilled
from its ponytail. It hung in a tangled mass around her
shoulders, tempting his fingers and evaporating all

thought of yelling at the woman. Her face flushed and, when her eyes met his, fire flickered in her dark orbs.

A knock sounded, and thankful for the interruption, he turned toward the doorway where Jim had appeared.

"Yeah?" Colt asked, stealing time to calm his nerves.

"Just wanted to let you know I'm gonna need Three in a chute so's I can work on him. Those cuts are pretty deep."

Colt struck his Stetson against his jeans. *Barbed wire.* It kept the cows where they belonged, but one loose strand was all it took to inflict serious damage. At least with the fencing, he could send one of the hands out into the pasture to gather it up. He glanced back at the woman who had flames in her eyes and anger on her lips.

Something told him ridding the ranch of downed wire would be a lot easier than getting Emma off the Circle P...or out of his head.

HOISTING HER DAUGHTER onto her hip, Emma turned to face the man whose yells had sent Bree into hysterics. The big rancher didn't even have the decency to look ashamed. Far too calmly, he lowered a glass of iced tea. He crowded her and Bree against the counter until all Emma could see were his wide shoulders and the anger that darkened his blue eyes.

"It's better she's a little scared than hurt," he growled. "Your daughter nearly got herself killed."

Immediately, he stepped back, ice cubes clinking against the glass as he gestured toward the barn.

Suddenly there were far too many pairs of widening eyes surrounding her and not enough air in a room that had gone cold despite the warm temperature.

"What?" Emma asked, not understanding and desperate for answers.

But Sarah only swooped in, prying Bree's unwilling fingers from around her neck.

"Come on, Bree," she said, her voice firm but cheery. "Ms. Doris and I were on our way to the greenhouse. Why don't you come with us? We'll look at the flowers. You can turn on the sprinklers."

Bree raised a tear-stained face. "Can I, Mommy?"

Emma brushed a hand over her daughter's damp features. The idea that Bree had been in danger was as earth-shattering as it was preposterous. Either way, Colt needed to know how badly he'd messed up. But facing down the cowboy was not something she wanted to do with an audience.

"You'll love it," she said, denying the tendril of fear that snaked across her midsection. "You go along with Ms. Sarah and Ms. Doris for a bit. When you come back, you can help me finish the dessert." Her gaze flicked to the armload of ingredients she'd spilled onto the counter in her haste to answer Bree's cries. A vague sense that something was missing from the haphazard pile of canned goods and staples tugged at her. She ignored the feeling while she narrowed in on the insolent man who stood in the kitchen calmly swirling ice in his glass, as if he hadn't just made her daughter cry.

No, the conversation she'd have with Colt Judd would not be fit for little ears.

The minute her two guardians escorted Bree out of sight, Emma crossed her arms and gave Colt her sternest look. "You had no right to yell at my child," she said, squelching the urge to give the man a dose of his own loud medicine. "She's just a little girl. What in heaven's name were you thinking?"

She waited while the big rancher set aside his glass, certain no excuse he could come up with would justify his actions.

"The bull got out."

"The bull?" Emma's breath caught in her throat. Her hands dropped to her sides. She reached behind her, clutching the counter for support.

She'd seen the huge animal this morning when four cowboys delivered it to the pen. Massive hooves. A thick, muscular body. An even heavier head. Its horns were so wide, not even a strapping figure of a man like Colt could touch both tips at the same time. Not that he'd ever get that close.

Only a fool would. A fool, or a child who didn't know any better.

She didn't need anyone to put two and two together to know the animal would make quick work of her inquisitive little girl.

"I wouldn't have let her out of my sight if I'd known…" She stopped herself. Her lips trembling, she met Colt's blue-eyed stare. "Thank you," she whispered. "Thank you for saving my daughter's life."

Colt's firm hand grasped her forearm. His soft voice cut through the white noise that filled her head.

"You probably didn't see many snakes or scorpions or wild coyotes in New York. Not many cows running loose there, either, I bet."

His words slowed. "Nine days out of ten, life on the ranch goes according to plan. But…" Colt nudged his hat away from the edge of the counter where he'd set it. "Every once in a while, something goes wrong. A cow breaks through a fence. Someone leaves the gate open at the end of the drive, and some of the herd wanders onto the highway." He shrugged. "A bull slips past a gate. When that happens, I'll do my best to fix things. That might mean raising my voice to get my point across."

Emma swallowed. There were situations—like the time Bree darted toward a busy street—that justified a quick, no-nonsense response.

"You were right," she conceded. Lest Colt think he was off the hook, she added, "Let's just not make a habit of it."

The atmosphere in the room thawed as every sign of anger dropped away from the rancher. He stepped back, loosening his hold on Emma's arm.

"Look." Apparently anxious to leave, he grabbed his hat and stuck it on his head. "I've got more on my plate than I'll finish today. But you and Bree need a crash course in ranching 101. Why don't I show you around tomorrow, right after Mom and the rest of the boys leave?"

Emma flexed her fingers, not that it did any good. Numbness spread from the spot where Colt's hand had left a big, warm imprint, right up her arm and into her brain. Blindly, she nodded. She watched until he left the room, uncertainty slowing her steps and muddling her thoughts. Though he'd made it clear he resented her presence on the Circle P, it sounded as if he might be willing to give her a chance. And a chance was all she needed.

One chance to prove she could handle the job. Starting now.

She hustled toward the ingredients she'd assembled for the cobbler. Once more the feeling that something wasn't right seeped through her. She gave the counter a closer look, her gaze stuttering to a stop on the empty book stand, where she'd propped the Circle P's cookbook.

Her heart sinking, she stepped closer.

The book lay facedown, one half on the counter, the other half hanging into the sink full of sudsy water.

"No," Emma whispered. "No. No. No."

Tears gathered in her eyes. She snatched the dripping notebook from the sink. Her cheeks grew damp as she stared at smears of blue ink, all that was left of the beloved recipes.

Colt had just proven he could fix nearly everything on the Circle P. He had saved her daughter from serious injury. Maybe worse. But even he had limits.

Emma groaned. It would take more than a big, strong, handsome cowboy to restore the treasured Circle P cookbook.

Chapter Four

Certain Emma's dark eyes traced his every step, Colt forced an extra bit of swagger into his walk. The move took every ounce of self-reassurance in his considerable arsenal, but he maintained the image until his boots struck the dirt at the end of the patio. Safely out of view from the kitchen windows, he sucked in a calming breath. Except drawing in a lungful of damp, hot air didn't exactly have the relaxing effect he hoped it would. Any more than curling and uncurling his fingers soothed the burning sensation that had sped up his hands and arms the moment he'd reached out to Emma. If anything, the deep breathing only spread a jittery sensation from his abdomen to points farther south, while flexing his fingers made them ache for another touch of soft skin.

And why the heck was that?

He neither wanted nor appreciated an attraction to the Circle P's newest employee. From the moment he'd first spotted the young cook standing on the front porch holding a fancied-up basket, she'd done nothing but infuriate him. So what if he'd snagged one of her cookies, and it was great. And, yeah, his mom thought well enough of the newcomer to put the Circle P's kitchen in her hands. None of that changed his initial impression. The way Emma had chastised him for raising his voice only added to his determination to make her stay on the Circle P a short one.

So why had a single touch triggered the same rushed reaction he'd left behind with his randy, teenage years?

Unable to answer the question and just as determined not to dwell on it, he trudged toward the barn. There, Ty and several hands had penned Three in a narrow chute more suited to the vet's business than an open corral. The men had better things to do, chores that weren't getting done, and the fault was all his. He should have known the bull's quirks and habits ahead of time. Should have pressed Josh for more information before he sent the young man off to repair a fence. It was what his dad would have done, and he vowed to do a better job of following in Seth's boot steps. Even if it meant studying the pedigree and history of each head of cattle on the ranch until the words swam before his eyes. Colt ran a hand through sweat-dampened hair and resettled his hat.

"That's the last stitch, big guy." Holding a large needle aloft, Jim stepped away from the chute. The vet headed for the back of his truck, where he stashed his bag, and grabbed more supplies. "Dose him with antibiotics every three days," he said, handing Colt a large syringe and a tube. "Smear this ointment over the affected area for the next ten days. After that, you should be able to cut him loose."

Colt ran a finger over his hat brim. "By then, we'll have solved our wire problem." Wanting the job done right, he singled out a worker who wasn't Josh. "Scour the brush all along the fence line. You find any loose wire, get rid of it."

"Yes, sir, boss." Whether the hand was eager to please or simply putting on a show in front of Ty, Colt didn't know and didn't care. He concentrated on smearing the cream on Three's sore hip before he nodded to the rest of the workers. "Let him out."

The moment the men released the bull, Three showed his appreciation for his new-found freedom by bucking his way around the larger pen. Colt noted the bull's shallow leaps, the halfhearted twists and turns.

"Definitely not rodeo material," he noted, propping his elbows on the top rail next to Ty's. The orneriest bulls had a bit of Brahman in them. Three was pure Andalusian.

"I'm pretty sure even I could cover him," said the man who'd never gone eight seconds in the ring. "But then, we don't raise rodeo stock. Speaking of which, that was quite a dustup earlier."

Colt scuffed his boot through the dirt. "Sorry about all the commotion."

"Wasn't the first time." Ty shrugged. "Won't be the last. You get everything straightened out?"

"I got my point across." Colt stared at a distant stand of palm trees. "Don't want to think what could have happened..." His hold on the rail tightened into the death grip he'd used on the rope back when he made his living by sitting atop of a ton of bucking bull.

"Good thing you were in the right place at the right time. Emma's new here. She'll learn." Ty leaned toward him. "Sarah and me, we faced the same kinds of problems when we first brought Jimmy to the ranch."

A slow breath eased between Colt's lips. Two years ago he'd already hung up his spurs and retired from the rodeo circuit. Back then, busy trying to prove he could handle the job as advance man for the PBR, he'd skipped the cattle drive that had resulted in a family for his friend.

"Jimmy snuck off while I was keepin' an eye on him," Ty continued. "Did the same thing to Sarah in the middle of a thunderstorm. Kids." He slipped a piece of straw between his teeth. "They do stuff without thinking. It's up to us to protect them from themselves."

"How'd you do that? With Jimmy, I mean." It wasn't his job to watch after Bree, but Ty and Sarah were the most attentive parents Colt had ever known. If they'd had trouble keeping track of a young'un, a single mom might, too.

"Time and patience," Ty said. "I kept him at my side as much as I could. Taught him what he needed to know. Things like, don't dive in until you know what else is in the water."

Colt kneaded his upper thigh. Not following that advice had nearly cost him a leg when he was eight. "Man, the trouble we got into when we were young. It's a wonder we survived."

"There was always a bunch of us around. The older ones," Ty said, with an elbow jab, "kept the little ones from doing stupid things."

"Or saved 'em when they did." Times had changed. His childhood pals were settling down with families of their own. Jimmy and Bree were the only children on the Circle P these days, and Ty's son would be in Hawaii for the next month or so. Which meant the burden for keeping Bree safe fell to him, Colt guessed. As if he didn't have enough responsibilities.

He pushed away from the railing. "I've got bills to handle and calls to make this afternoon, but I'm giving Emma and her daughter the fifty-cent tour tomorrow.

I'll make sure they know what to watch out for." Coyotes and the occasional bobcat roamed the pastures. Alligators frequented the pond out back. Snakes and scorpions put in routine appearances.

Ty shoved off, too. "I better get moving myself. We need to get on the road if Sarah's going to drop by the Department of Children and Families office before it closes." The Circle P's owners planned to spend the night in the city before catching an early morning flight.

"You looking to foster another child?" Colt asked as they cut across the yard. Unlike most foster parents, Ty and Sarah provided a permanent, stable home for the kids in their care. They had room, now that Tim and Chris had grown, to take in another child or two.

"Maybe. After we get back."

They split up in the foyer. Colt waited until Ty bounded up the stairs to the master bedroom before he headed for the office. On his way, a sudden thirst that didn't have anything to do with wanting to see their new cook again propelled him toward the kitchen. At the threshold, he halted.

Emma stood across the room, her back to him. His gaze climbed past her denim-clad legs, skimmed over a tiny, cinched-in waist and landed on shaking shoulders. She bent over the sink, one hand repeatedly skimming the surface of the water. Unease whispered through him. With it came the realization that their new cook was crying. He stepped into the room, quietly pulling the kitchen door closed behind him. Four long strides brought him close enough to make out her words.

"Oh, no. Oh, no. Oh, no."

Was she hurt? Had something happened to Bree? "Emma," he called softly.

Silence.

She spun away from the sink, horror and fear swimming in her eyes, crumpled wet paper in one fist. With her other hand, she pressed a pulpy mass to her chest. For a second, Colt stood riveted by the gut-wrenching tears that spilled from her dark eyes. The droplets left tracks on her blotchy cheeks. He steeled himself and peered past her to the counter. Canisters, bowls and wooden spoons littered the work space.

No blood, he noted. *So far, so good.*

Water splashed onto the tip of his boot. He stepped back, his stomach lurching as he spotted a familiar design on the leather cover of a soggy book. His focus shifted to Emma's open palm, where he barely recognized his mother's handwriting smeared across the drenched paper.

Anger, white and hot, blinded him.

"Emma," he demanded, his voice hoarse, "what have you done?"

Run! Hide!

The words reverberated while Emma stood, frozen, unable to speak, much less able to move. Colt's harsh whisper broke through her mind-numbing panic.

"It was... It was an accident," she stammered. Her chest squeezed when she dared to look up at him. A strangled mix of pain and fury spread across the rancher's features. Wishing there was something, anything, she could do to erase it, she had nothing.

"How bad is it?" he demanded through clenched teeth.

"Awful." She placed the ruined notebook in his outstretched hands. Though the back half remained intact, the front was all sodden paper and smeared ink. A muscle along Colt's jaw twitched. Emma braced for a torrent of angry words. For the crash of thrown dishes and pots and pans. For accusations, raised hands. She studied the waterlogged mess he held. "What can I do?"

He peered up from wringing-wet pages. "I think you've done enough, don't you?"

No matter how well deserved, the caustic retort stung. She searched for an appropriate response, was still searching when someone knocked on the door to the hallway. Muffled by thick wood, Doris's voice drifted into the room.

"Who closed this door?" The knob rattled and something thumped. "Darn thing's jammed. Emma? Tim? Chris? You in there? Open up."

Emma's heart stuttered. Surprised when Colt didn't stride to the door in his eagerness to spill the news, she shot the tall rancher a questioning look. For the first time since they'd met, doubt and indecision played across his chiseled features. He stared down at the ruined pages.

"This'll kill her." His voice thinned. "We can't let her find out."

When another thump sounded at the door, the soggy mess landed back in Emma's grasp.

"Put it…somewhere," Colt hissed.

His wide hand at Emma's waist propelled her behind him. Shielded by Colt's broad shoulders, she spread the damp mass on the counter and covered it with a towel. She'd no more than finished when the door popped open. She and Colt spun away from the sink as Doris stumbled across the threshold and into the kitchen.

"Mom, are you okay?" Colt hurried to her side.

"Of course I'm all right. Why wouldn't I be?"

While Colt blocked his mother's view, Emma gave the counter a quick look. She swallowed a relieved sigh when she didn't spot so much as a scrap of paper.

"Why'd you close the door? You know the humidity makes it swell."

"That was my fault, Doris," Emma offered. "I was working on tonight's dessert and didn't want to be interrupted."

"Oh? Something special?" The top of Doris's gray head barely appeared beyond Colt's shoulder before he shifted to block her view.

"Don't be nosy, Mom," Colt said smoothly. "You'll ruin the surprise." He draped his arm around his mother's shoulders and steered her back the way she'd come. "You'll just have to wait and see. Now, can I get you anything? Some tea? A snack?"

"Hold on just a minute." Emma caught the merest glimpse of Doris peering up at her son. "I need to go over the shopping schedule with our new cook. Make sure she has the next supply order ready on time."

"We make the run to Okeechobee each Thursday," Colt said as if reciting from a list. "To the big-box store over on the coast the first Tuesday of every month. The butcher delivers on Fridays. We call to place that order by Wednesday." He shrugged one shoulder. "Ty and I went over everything last night. I'll fill Emma in. It's part of my job."

Doris patted her son's arm. "Sounds like you'll do just fine. Your dad would be so proud."

It was a good thing Colt snaked his arms around his mother and drew her close. Otherwise, a woman as sharp as Doris would have noticed the stricken look that formed on the tall man's face. "I'm sure there'll be some hiccups," he said in a strangled tone that made Emma's heart ache, "but you're only a phone call away. I'll get in touch if I need to."

Appeased, Doris started to leave. At the door, she hesitated and stepped back toward them. "Did I answer all your questions, Emma? Was there anything else you needed?"

Know a good restoration specialist?

She swallowed. "You don't have a thing to worry about." Though it pained her to lie to the older woman, she understood Colt's decision to keep the damage under wraps. Or at least, she thought she did.

The minute his mother's footsteps faded down the hall, Colt turned to face her. Gone was the softness he'd shown Doris. Looking at features that were all hard angles and angry glints, Emma knew the time had come. From the second she'd lifted the waterlogged cookbook from its bath, she'd known her dreams of making a home on the Circle P had ended. No apologies would ever be enough. No amount of begging or pleading would earn her a second chance. The how or why wouldn't matter. Nothing could change the fact that she'd destroyed a family heirloom. She'd have to leave.

"I'll go. First thing tomorrow. Tonight, if you'd rather."

Colt's blank stare swam into focus. He shook his head. "Oh, no. You're not getting off that easy. You made this mess. It's up to you to stay and help fix it."

Emma quickly snuffed out a wisp of hope. She folded her arms across her chest. "How exactly do you propose

I do that, Colt? I don't even know what half those recipes were. Much less how to prepare them."

"I do. I grew up eating my mom's cooking. I bet I've had every dish in that book a dozen times or more. You're some kind of fancy New York chef." He jabbed a finger in her direction. "I'll describe what something looks like, how it tastes. You'll fix it."

"If only it were that simple." She sighed. "Re-creating those recipes will involve trial and error. Lots of it." Mostly error, she imagined, unless Colt knew more about spices and seasoning than she thought he did.

The big man raised his hands in a sign of surrender. "We have eight or nine months till I leave when Randy and Royce take over. That ought to be time enough."

Work together?

"I don't know…" Emma hedged.

"Do we have any choice? It's either that or tell my mom what really happened, and I think both of us know what'll happen then."

Emma didn't need him to spell it out for her. Instead of taking some much-needed time away from the ranch, Doris would insist on staying put. Garrett and Arlene wouldn't get the help they needed. As for herself, she'd lose her job and, without references, any hope of giving her daughter a secure future.

She scanned the huge kitchen with its wide counters and enormous center island. Not even a space this large was big enough to let her keep her distance from the man who threatened her equilibrium in ways no one ever had before. But it was up to her to make things right. If that meant spending night after night working with Colt, she had to do it.

"Okay," she agreed at last.

Relief softened Colt's hard edges. "Okay," he repeated. "For now, we need to salvage what we can. I can't take this mess to my room. Garrett'll spot it in a heartbeat, and by the next one, the whole ranch will know what happened." He grabbed a roll of paper towels and handed them to her. "Place several sheets between the wet pages. It'll wick most of the water out."

"And if it doesn't?"

He kneaded his fist against his palm. "You and I will sit down tomorrow night and figure out what's missing. Till then, we can't let anyone find out what's happened. Ty and Sarah are leaving in a little while. Mom and my brothers, in the morning. We only have to keep this a secret until then."

As plans went, this one had some pretty big gaps. "I don't know. I'm not sure any of this is a good idea."

"You have a better suggestion?" he challenged.

Despite what had to be the world's worst timing, desire shivered below her waist when he pinned her with an intense look. She shook her head, denying her attraction to the tall rancher while she admitted he was right.

"I thought not," he grumbled, looking away.

Minutes later, her back pressed against her bedroom door's hard wooden surface, Emma struggled to catch her breath while the implications of this latest disaster crashed around her shoulders. Her gaze swept over cedar-planked walls, photographs taken at various rodeos, the usual assortment of bedroom furniture. Tears gathered in her eyes.

She'd planned to help secure the ranch's reputation as a travel destination while her daughter thrived in Florida's fresh air and sunshine. Instead, a rampaging bull had nearly trampled Bree. The cookbook the Circle P had staked its reputation on was in tatters. Even more disturbing, this latest run-in with Colt had shaken her opinion of the rancher. On the surface, he came across like every other Mr. Wrong she'd ever known—bold, arrogant, bossy.

During their talk this morning and later with his mom, she'd sensed a softer side lay beneath Colt's gruff exterior. One he worked hard to keep hidden. Oh, he was angry with her, no doubt about that. And rightfully so. But rather than explode into a rage, he'd tempered his emotions. For his mother's sake, he'd given her another chance. Determined to make it a good one, Emma wiped her eyes, ran a hand through her hair and peered down at the cookbook, hoping things weren't as bad as she feared.

No such luck.

With frequent breaks to blot her cheeks lest her tears make things worse, she removed the loose pages and layered paper towels between the damp ones. At last, she spread more towels atop the desk and fanned what was left of the notebook wide open so it could dry. Having done all she could for the moment, Emma sat back. A soggy ball of pulp was all that was left of at least a dozen recipes. The writing on another third of the book had smeared, turning directions that were barely decipherable to begin with into incomprehensible gibberish. It was ludicrous to think she and Colt could carry out his plan, and she glanced toward the closet where she'd stashed her suitcases.

Rapid footsteps on the stairs put any decisions on hold. Emma crossed to the door, just as her daughter bounded into the room. All thin arms and churning legs, Bree slammed into her.

"Mommy, I brought you a flower." Breathless, Bree held out her prize. "Miz Sarah, she grows them in a big house all of their own. She calls it a green house, but it isn't green. It's white. Why do they call it green when it isn't, Mommy?" Bree's head swung to the desk. "What's that?"

"My book got all wet," Emma explained. "I'm trying to dry it."

Bree's little fingers reached out to the wet paper. Damp edges smeared into nothingness at her touch.

"Careful, baby." Emma tucked Bree's hand in hers. "We want to save as much as we can."

"You should get a new one," her daughter declared with the surety of youth.

"I wish I could," Emma confessed. "But it's the only one like it. I have to fix as much as I can before anyone finds out."

Bree's head tilted up, her eyes widening. "Is it a secret, Mommy?" She brought one finger to her lips. "Shh. I won't tell."

Emma's eyes narrowed. *A secret?*

She stared out the window. Eventually, the truth would come out. Probably sooner rather than later, she'd have to come clean about the ruined cookbook.

But the delay would give Doris a chance to visit with her pregnant daughter-in-law. It would give Bree the opportunity to learn there was more to life than sidewalks and busy streets. In the meantime, she'd circulate her résumé against the day a certain hunky cowboy changed his mind about keeping her on at the Circle P.

Her decision made, Emma gave Bree a hug. "What say we let this dry for now while we go make the apple cobbler for tonight's dessert." The recipe for that dish had been safely tucked in her pocket throughout the whole disastrous afternoon. She took her daughter's hand.

Long before dinner, the delicious odor of apples and cinnamon filled the house and spilled from the kitchen into the yard. Much to Bree's delight, ravenous cowboys filed in soon after Emma rang the bell. While Bree watched, they devoured platters of bread and salad, and helped themselves to bowls of piping hot stew.

In the dining room, where she and Bree joined the family, Emma kept her expression blank as Hank frowned down at his bowl.

"What is this?" he asked, his nose wrinkling.

She tried not to squirm as several pairs of eyes turned her way.

"Now, don't you boys start in on Emma. This isn't hers." Doris spooned some of the thin broth. "Stacy Gillmore sent it."

"Not as good as yours, Mom," Garrett pronounced.

"Yeah." Royce swallowed a bite. "Yours is—"

"—better," Randy finished. "This is more like soup."

Emma caught Doris's knowing glance.

"Brunswick stew is a huge favorite on the cattle drives." Doris sampled another bite. "Mine's thicker," she said after a bit. "The recipe's in the book."

"Good to know." Emma stared at her bowl. All that remained of the soups and stews section were a few pulpy scraps. "You know, I keep all my favorites on my laptop. Did you ever consider—"

Across the table, Colt's head rose expectantly.

"A computer?" Doris fanned herself. "Mercy, no. Sarah's a whiz with them, but I know just enough to get into trouble. Email's about all I can manage. That's how I stay in touch with these two." She pointed to Royce and Randy.

Colt slumped in his chair, refusing to meet her eyes. Emma stirred a fork through her bowl of watery stew. She and the rancher faced an impossible task. One that wasn't going to get any easier if Colt couldn't even bear to look at her.

Chapter Five

A low buzz of conversation drifted in from the kitchen. Colt caught the shuffle of boot heels against the tiled floor. He swirled his fork through a bowl of tasteless stew while someone in the other room rattled silverware in a drawer. Probably one of the ranch hands looking for a serving spoon. The way his luck was running, they'd polish off the pan of apple-whatever that had looked and smelled so tempting he'd nearly helped himself to a dish on his way to the dining room. He licked his lips. For once, he wished he'd skipped dinner and gone straight to dessert.

The ice cubes in his glass shifted, their harsh clinks a reminder that wishes didn't always come true. If they did, his dad would be seated at the head of the table. His mom wouldn't be leaving her home of nearly forty years. The Circle P's cookbook would still be intact. And his life would go back to the way it had always been.

Except for the scrape of silverware against plates, the dining room remained depressingly silent. Garrett had spent hours on the phone with Arlene this afternoon. The worry lines etched into his brother's forehead told Colt that the most recent doctor's appointment hadn't gone any better than the one before it. Hank had kept to himself all day. He claimed a real estate closing had kept him busy, but Colt had seen his brother take off on horseback around two. He'd returned wrapped in a sullen blanket of withdrawal, the same one he'd worn after he and the Tompkins girl called it quits their senior year of high school. As for Randy and Royce, the duo had walked around with glum expressions on their faces ever since their return from the little house.

Colt fought the urge to scratch his head. His family deserved more than this for their last night together, though, so far, he hadn't come up with a better plan. No more than he could figure out why his mom had insisted the new cook and her daughter join them at the dinner table. Emma had only been on the ranch for two days. Yet she'd already developed an irritating habit of getting under his skin.

He should have fired her when he had the chance.

She'd certainly given him plenty of reason to escort her to the end of the property and wave goodbye. Instead, he'd covered for her, all but guaranteeing he'd have to work with her to restore the Circle P's collection of recipes before anyone found out it'd been damaged.

He tried not to stare, but that proved even more difficult than looking interested in his food. A few tendrils had escaped Emma's ponytail. They curled softly on her neck, framing a face that was more interesting than it was beautiful. Sooty lashes brushed her cheeks, but he knew beneath those lowered lids were the kind of eyes a man could get lost in. Something he'd nearly done in the kitchen this afternoon.

For the life of him, he couldn't figure out why every time he came within ten feet of the woman, he wanted to sling a protective arm around her shoulders. And then there was her daughter. He didn't have much experience with youngsters. Back when he was on the rodeo circuit, most of the riders weren't much more than kids themselves. Lately, he'd had even less interaction with the preschool set. Oh, occasionally one interrupted his meal in a restaurant. Or he spotted a harried mother and her brood when he stopped to pick up supplies. But it didn't happen often enough to rub the edge off his curiosity.

At Emma's side, Bree speared a carrot, which she lifted, wet and dripping, from her bowl. She plunked it down on her bread plate. Without looking up, she carefully scraped off every drop of brown sauce. Only then did she take a tentative bite. Her elfin face scrunched. Her nose wrinkled. With obvious distaste, she slid the offending vegetable back in the bowl.

Colt swallowed a chuckle. He didn't care much for the dish himself. He rubbed his midsection, where the few bites he'd managed to force down refused to settle. With her long curly hair and big dark eyes, he thought Bree might look a lot like her mom when she got older. Not that he'd ever know. He didn't plan to stick around long enough to see the child start first grade, much less graduate from high school. When a lump rose in his throat, he cleared it and snagged a roll from the overflowing basket Emma had placed on the table.

"It's good that Ty and Sarah went ahead with their trip." The owners had said their goodbyes earlier. He spread a liberal helping of butter across soft dough. "What about everyone else? When are you taking off?"

"Five?" Garrett suggested while Doris's gaze drifted beyond the suitcases piled by the front door. "Maybe six? I'd like to be home before dark."

Emma glanced up from her dish. "Do you want breakfast before you go?" she asked, her voice a mere whisper.

"Just coffee." Garrett checked the cell phone he'd kept at his side all afternoon. "We'll hit a drive-through when we stop for gas." He paused as if he suddenly remembered his traveling companion. "If that's okay with you, Mom."

"What?" With visible effort, Doris steered her attention back to the conversation. "Oh, sure. Fine. Whatever you want." She traced each twist of her thick braid the way a supplicant fingered rosary beads.

Colt tracked his mom's wandering interest. When he realized she'd been staring down the hall toward the bedroom she and his dad had shared, the tasty roll lost its flavor. He lowered the uneaten half to a plate. "Hank?" He swallowed. "How 'bout you?"

The younger Judd swiped a finger across the calendar on his smartphone. "The rest of us fly out of West Palm. We'll leave the same time as Garrett." He glanced at Emma. "Randy, Royce and me'll grab a bite at the airport."

"You'll need a driver. I'll send Josh." The ranch hand had to be good for something besides reading while he held up the side of a barn. "If you need anything from the grocery store—" Colt gave Emma a pointed look "—let him know. He can stop and pick things up on his way home."

"More paper towels." Emma took a bite without meeting his eyes.

Beside her, Bree's head lifted. A breathless anticipation filling the little girl's voice, she whispered, "Mommy…"

"Shh, baby." Emma wrapped one arm around her daughter's waist. "Remember what we talked about upstairs."

Colt's gaze shifted from daughter to mother. Even a novice at handling kids could tell the little girl had a secret—*their* secret—and wasn't doing an especially good job of keeping it. He speared a chunk of meat from his bowl and chomped down on a piece of beef that tasted like old leather and took just as much effort to chew. He made a face just as Bree looked up from the vegetables she'd been chasing around her plate without managing to catch a single one.

The little girl's giggles broke the heavy silence.

"Bree." Emma whispered a warning, and Bree clapped a hand over her mouth.

The lines on Doris's face softened. "I miss that sound—children laughing at the table. Nothing else does a body that much good."

Sensing he was onto something, Colt stood his half-eaten roll on end and, using his forefinger, pretended to kick it through an invisible goal post. His brothers smiled when Bree laughed out loud. One by one, they got in on the act, each trying to outdo the other in their efforts to put a smile on their mom's face.

"Knock, knock," Royce said when it was his turn.

"Who's there?" Bree squirmed forward on her chair, her eyes bright.

"Amos," chimed Randy.

"Amos, who?" Bree followed the lines that bounced between the twins.

"A mosquito bit me." Royce laughed.

"And it was this big." Randy spread his arms so wide he jostled Hank's elbow.

Meat and vegetables clung perilously to Hank's fork before they plunged into his lap.

"Randy, you clumsy oaf!" Hank swore and sprang

to his feet. "Now look what you've done." Brushing at gravy smeared on his jeans, he strode from the room.

Emma's fork clattered into her bowl. Colt's stomach tightened at the stricken look that crossed her face. Her movements brusque, she pushed away from the table.

"Excuse us. Bree and I will take our plates to the kitchen." She gave her daughter's hand a tug. "Come on, honey. It's time for bed."

"But, Mommy, I'm not tired." The laughter that had danced in Bree's eyes dimmed.

Colt frowned. The guys had only been teasing one another, the same way they usually did. So they got a little carried away. So what? It wouldn't be the first time. Propping his elbows on the edge of the table, he pinned Emma with a pointed look. "Might get a bit too noisy for sleeping. The bunch of us—" he pointed a finger at his brothers "—we're gonna jam after supper. You're welcome to sit in. Bree, too."

"We are?" Hank emerged from the kitchen, a dish towel pressed against his pants leg.

Having announced it to the group, Colt felt certain he'd hit on just what the family needed. They all missed Dad. His absence filled the room. But it was time to make some new memories, ones that would carry them into the future and draw them back home when the time came.

As if she'd read his mind, Doris chimed in. "Your father wouldn't want us to sit around moping. He'd tell us to laugh, sing, enjoy life."

That sounded exactly like something his dad would say, and Colt nodded to his mom. "You'll join in?" He'd never mastered an instrument, but she'd taught him to sing harmony when he wasn't much older than Bree.

"It'll be like old times." Doris lowered her fork. She pushed her plate away.

Not exactly, Colt thought, but he turned to Garrett. "You haven't forgotten how to play, have you?"

"I didn't bring my guitar." The eldest of the brothers nodded toward one that hung from pegs in the great room. "Think Ty would mind if I borrowed his?"

"Of course not." Colt turned to the twins. "Royce, Randy—you in?"

Randy scooched his chair back. "I'll get my harmonica," he said, rising.

Royce lifted two spoons from the table. He clapped them against the flat of his hand. "These'll do," he said.

Colt caught the furtive looks his brothers sent toward the fireplace and the stand that held their dad's banjo. An awkward moment passed when Hank crossed to the instrument. He plucked the strings.

"I'm not nearly as good as Dad." He toed one boot against the floor. "But I guess I can pick a little."

"You've been holding out on us?" Warmth spread from Colt's lips to his eyes. He was onto Hank's ways. Only an accomplished player claimed to pick *a little.* "Sounds like we're all set, then. Emma, how 'bout you and Bree?" He aimed a wide, teasing grin toward the little girl whose fingers were too tiny to stretch across the guitar frets.

Firmly, Emma shook her head. "I'm afraid not." She stacked Bree's bowl atop hers. Her shoulders stiff and unyielding, she marched out of the room.

Around the table, the brothers held their collective breaths when Doris's expression crumpled into dismayed lines. "Well, maybe we shouldn't…" she began.

"Hold that thought." Colt swiped his napkin across

his mouth. "I'll talk to her. The rest of you get tuned up. Royce—" he nodded toward the younger twin "—maybe you can show Bree how you tap those spoons."

In an instant, Bree scooted to the twin's side. "Let me see!" Her eyes widening, she followed his every move.

Colt grabbed his dinner dishes and headed for the kitchen. A night of music and songs would do them all so much good he couldn't let Emma squelch the idea. He no sooner stepped across the threshold than the young cook swung away from the trash can. His stomach clenched when she leaned against the counter as if bracing for an angry torrent.

"I know you hate waste but—"

"—but sometimes it can't be helped," Colt finished. Crossing the room, he emptied food he'd barely touched into the garbage can. He squinted into Emma's doubt-filled eyes. "What's got you all riled up?"

She waved a spoon as if trying to ward him off. "I don't have any idea what you're talking about."

"C'mon now, gal." Colt pointed out the obvious. "You gotta realize you jump quicker than a cottontail in a rattlesnake den whenever someone raises their voice. You want to tell me what's going on?" He stepped close enough to catch a whiff of spicy floral scent far more tantalizing than their meal.

"I do not," Emma protested, though her fingers shook so badly the dishes rattled as she placed them on the counter.

Cupping his hands over hers, he softened his tone to a near whisper. "Yeah, you kinda do. When you work on a ranch with a bunch of men, that's gonna be a problem. We yell. We holler. We might even cuss from time to time. If you run off every time someone shouts, pretty soon you're gonna hit the ocean." Hoping to put her at ease, he threw in his best aw-shucks grin. "This is Florida, you know."

Instead of smiling in return, Emma slipped her fingers from his grasp. She folded her arms across her chest and gave him a long, appraising look. "My dad was a drill sergeant. He ran our house the same way he ran his platoon. To escape, I got married, but my husband turned into a carbon copy of my father. I gave up any hope of ever making a name for myself when I found out most head chefs turn screaming at their assistants into an art form." She sighed. "I'm done with all that. A calm, quiet atmosphere—that's what your folks promised when I came here. They made the Circle P sound like something just this side of heaven."

Colt drummed his fingers on the counter. "It can be. We still have our moments." He nudged a stack of plates back from the edge. "You and I have had a few already," he acknowledged. "We met under awful circumstances. Bree's near miss with Three—that probably cost me a few gray hairs. As for what happened this afternoon—" he gestured toward the sink "—I'm normally not the type to ride roughshod over the hired help. So far, you haven't exactly seen me at my best, but things'll get better."

The firm set of Emma's mouth relaxed the tiniest bit. "You're turning into someone I didn't expect, Colt."

"Well, now. That's a good thing, isn't it?" His smile broadened. For a second or two, he thought he'd gotten through to her, convinced her he wasn't the bad guy she'd made him out to be. At the last moment, her face shuttered.

"I have work to do," she announced.

Colt followed her gaze around the kitchen. Though the ranch hands had done a passable job of cleaning up after themselves, serving dishes remained on the table. A few pots cluttered the stove. A pan on the counter snagged his attention. Bits of apple and crust clung to the sides. From the looks of things, the men hadn't saved even a bite of dessert for the family. He rubbed a hand over his empty stomach.

"This evening is more for Mom than anyone. It'd be really nice if you sat with us for a while."

Emma canted her head. "If I finish in here in time," she conceded.

He didn't quite understand why it was so important that Emma see him in a better light. He just knew that it was. But one look at her face told him not to waste his breath trying for anything more. He shrugged. The next few months would give him plenty of opportunity to prove he wasn't like the other men in her life. As he turned and walked away, determined to make the best of the last night with his family, the smile that flirted at the corners of his mouth had little to do with music and everything to do with what lay ahead.

As much as Emma told herself watching the big rancher disappear into the living room was a bad idea, she couldn't help it. She had to look. Had to see those wide shoulders and lean, muscular legs head in the opposite direction when what she really wanted was to have Colt take her in his arms and kiss her senseless.

Get a grip, she told herself.

The promise of a good job, a stable home and a great work environment had drawn her to the Circle P. Her recipe for future happiness didn't include anything more.

Certainly not a flirtation with someone as arrogant and bossy as Colt.

And yet…

There was another side to him. A side that didn't mesh with her first impression of the man who'd ordered her off the front porch and around to the servants' entrance. Yes, he'd been angry when she doused the family cookbook but, under the circumstances, who could blame him? He sure hadn't reacted like her father or her late husband. Both of *them* would have blurted out the truth without giving Doris's feelings a second thought. Besides, it was hard to find fault with the man who'd literally saved her daughter's life.

Stacking the dirty dishes beside the sink, she shook her head. No. She might be a great cook, but Colt's plan to re-create four generations of recipes through trial and error simply wouldn't work. No matter how many nights they spent in the kitchen, some of those recipes were lost forever.

She stifled a groan while, in the other room, Randy ran the scale on his harmonica. Garrett and Hank brushed the strings on instruments that, even to her untrained ears, sounded seriously out of tune. If that was the best they could do, it was going to be a long night. The cacophony of a dozen cats outside her bedroom window would sound better. To drown out the noise, she grabbed the first empty pot, plunged it beneath the soap suds and began scrubbing.

Minutes later, Bree burst into the kitchen. "Mommy! We're makin' music! Not music from the radio or the iPod. *Real* music. Come see!"

"Really?" Emma swiped at the gleaming counter. Seeing the delight in her daughter's eyes, she realized

the group in the living room *had* gotten their act together. For the past few minutes, she'd been tapping
her toe in time to the beat. She took a moment to steady
her voice. Before Jack died, they'd barely squeaked by
on his military pay. Afterward, between rent and baby-
sitters and culinary school, she hadn't had two nickels
to spare on such niceties as music lessons for a four-
year-old. Wasn't this one of the reasons she'd come to
the Circle P? To give Bree new experiences, ones she
couldn't have elsewhere?

She pulled out a pan of apple cobbler she'd kept hidden in the warming oven. "Well, let's go see. Will you
carry the ice cream?"

In the dining room, Bree paused only long enough to
dump the container on the table before she scrambled
straight into Colt's lap. The sight of her tiny little girl
wrapped in the rancher's tanned, muscular arms ignited
a warm spot in Emma's heart. One that expanded when
he guided the child's little hands in counting out the beat
for the next number.

"That's right. Just like you did before." *Tap. Tap. Tap.*
"Ready? Now…" In a clear tenor, he sang a funny song
about crawdads.

Colt really was full of surprises, she decided, listening to him lead the group in another verse. When Bree's
voice joined the others in singing the chorus, she felt
her heart melt.

"Did you like it, Mommy?" Bree asked when the last
notes faded. "Mr. Colt teached me."

Emma met the rancher's gaze and instantly got lost
in his blue eyes. "He taught me," she corrected.

"Did he teach you, too, Mommy?" Bree tilted her
head. "Will you sing your song?"

While the snippet of conversation drew laughter from the rest of Colt's family, it sent a flush of heat straight up the back of Emma's neck. In an effort to hide her rapidly warming face, she bent over the dessert plates while Garrett segued into the next number. Another song followed before they broke for apple cobbler and ice cream. By then, it seemed as if everyone was having such a good time no one wanted to call it quits. But, even excited four-year-olds had their limits, and shortly after dessert, Bree hit hers. She leaned her little head back against Colt's wide chest. Before the group finished their next song, she'd gone out like the proverbial light.

Emma stood. Colt rose at the same time.

"I'll carry her up for you."

"No." Simple, straightforward. The refusal flew from her mouth before she gave it a second thought. Colt's dark eyebrows buckled together as she practically wrenched her daughter from his grasp. But she couldn't let him come to her room. As much as she appreciated his offer to carry her child up the stairs, seeing him in this new light was seriously undermining her impression of the rancher. A new rush of emotions unsettled her, made her feel vulnerable.

"I've got her," she insisted.

Aware that Colt's brothers were staring at her, Emma wished she hadn't been so abrupt. But some things weren't meant to happen, and falling for a big, hunky cowboy wasn't any more likely than making a permanent home on the Circle P. As much as she wanted one and resisted the other, she'd have to keep her guard up or losing both would break her heart.

Chapter Six

Skirting shapes that loomed out of the darkness, Emma quietly padded through the house. She made her way to the kitchen, where she flipped the switch on the coffeepot she'd readied the night before. A yawn rippled through her, and she made a mental note to ask Colt about putting the brewer on a timer. Surely his demand for preserving tradition would bend that much, wouldn't it? Wondering what he'd say if he discovered that his mom had already abandoned at least one of the customs he deemed so important, she pulled several cans from the refrigerator's bottom drawer and quickly arranged biscuits on baking trays. They were ready for the oven by the time water boiled on the mammoth stove for her own cup of tea.

As a familiar warm scent gurgled from the battered percolator, Emma checked her watch and wiped sleep from her eyes. Her mug in her hand, she backtracked through the silent house, stepping onto the front porch without making a sound. A cathedral-like hush filled air that had cooled overnight. Mist drifted across land that was flatter than the thinnest pancake. Pinks and grays streaked the horizon as she settled into one of the rocking chairs to watch the sun rise.

She'd hardly taken her seat before a car engine broke

the stillness. She followed the sound toward the long driveway, where twin beams of lights flickered through a copse of trees. Ranch hands, she decided, sipping her tea. She wondered whether they were getting an early start on the day, or bringing a late night to an end.

But more cars followed the first until a train of headlights snaked from the main road toward the house. One by one, vehicles pulled into the parking area. Hinges protested. Dome lights winked on and off. Emma caught the murmur of hushed greetings and one hearty "Hey, man." From nearby trees, birds twittered their displeasure at being disturbed. Someone lit a match. The acrid scent of cigarette smoke tickled her nose. Unable to make out details, she counted silhouettes until she reached a dozen.

She abandoned her tea. Intent on telling someone— anyone—they had company, she slipped into the house. She paused at the door only long enough to wish she'd turned on a light to dispel some of the darkness. Heading in the general direction of the stairs, she took two steps before she collided with a solid body.

"Ooph," she gasped, inhaling a soapy fragrance accompanied by a uniquely masculine scent. Strong fingers grasped her upper arms.

"Steady there."

Colt's strong fingers, she corrected. His low timbre reverberated through her. A sharp awareness plunged into her midsection. Her hands rose. Traitors, they sought purchase on his muscular chest. For one long, delicious second, she clung to him before she reeled back.

"Sorry, sorry." Branded by his touch, she wrenched out of his grasp. "I, uh, I…"

"You all right? I didn't step on your toes or anything, did I?"

"I'm fine." Emma forced a sternness she didn't feel into her voice. Tugging, straightening, she ran a hand down her front. "Why were you lurking in the dark like that?"

"Heard a door slam. Thought I'd better check it out. What are *you* doing up so early?"

She registered the accusation in his tone and bristled. "We need a timer for the coffeepot. I had to set my alarm so it'd be ready." She struggled to remember why she was standing so close to Colt. In the dark. Alone. "There's quite a crowd outside."

"Probably the neighbors," he answered, as if the gathering was perfectly normal. "They've come to see Mom off. She and the rest of 'em are stirring. They'll be ready to leave soon. You say there's coffee? How 'bout rustling up a cup while I pay my respects. Two sugars. No cream."

The idea that half the town had turned out to usher Doris into the next stage of her life was so foreign, Emma ignored the fact that she'd just been ordered to fetch the man a drink. Though everyone said the military was a close-knit community, she couldn't recall a single time when friends of her parents had shown up to wish them well on their next post. It certainly hadn't happened during her short-lived marriage. As for building relationships in New York, forget about it. Between raising a baby on her own and an impossible workload, she doubted her neighbors there even knew her name, much less where she was headed when she moved out.

She shifted her weight from one leg to the other while she considered what it'd be like to have the kind of roots Colt and his family had on the Circle P. In a community where people cared so much about one another they rolled out of bed before daybreak to see them off. It was the life she'd dreamed of when she accepted the job on the ranch. The one she wanted for her daughter and, to be honest, for herself. Could she still have it? Staring at the spot Colt had vacated, she vowed to try.

In the kitchen, she poured coffee and loaded a tray with sweeteners and milk. By the time she made it to the front of the house again, Garrett had finished loading suitcases into an economical sedan. His brothers were tossing boxes and duffel bags into the back of one of the Circle P's trucks.

A sudden awareness of how much she didn't fit in with the group assailed her. Not wanting to intrude, she made up her mind to grab her tea and duck back inside. But she hadn't planned on Doris. Stepping onto the porch, the older woman wrapped her in a warm embrace.

"Emma," Doris whispered in her ear. "Thanks for last night. We enjoyed it so much." She pulled away to glance at the empty spot at Emma's side. "How's our little girl this morning?"

"Still fast asleep." A tired child was a cranky child, and Bree had stayed up far past her usual bedtime. "She'll be sorry she missed all this." Emma waved a hand at the crowd that lined the walkway from the porch to Garrett's car.

Doris's lined face crinkled. "It's quite the send-off, isn't it? But I can leave easy, knowing the kitchen's in good hands."

"I wish I felt as sure about that as you do." The urge to confess beat frantically against her ribs. Emma swallowed. No matter how many reasons she gave herself for keeping her secret, she couldn't overlook one fact— Doris deserved to hear the truth. Today. Before she left.

"Listen," Emma started, "I, um, there's something you should know."

Doris's smile froze. The first shimmer of doubt wavered in her eyes just as a heavy hand clamped down on Emma's shoulder.

"You ready to go, Mom? Garrett's already spoken with Arlene this morning. She says she can't wait for you to get there."

In the pale morning light, Emma read the warning in Colt's blue eyes. She wrenched her gaze from his, only to spot Garrett leaning against his car, one foot tapping impatiently. A plume of smoke rose from the truck's tailpipe. Josh sat behind the wheel, waiting while Hank and the twins checked the tie-downs in the back. And in between stood half the population of Glades County.

Emma sighed. Her confession wouldn't fix a thing. It would only derail everyone's plans. She summoned a smile.

"I can't promise that I'll do everything the same way you did, Doris, but I'll keep everyone fed."

"That's all anyone can ask." Doris leaned in for a final squeeze.

"C'mon, Mom. Everybody's waitin'." Colt's hand slipped from Emma's shoulder to his mother's elbow.

Showing far more tenderness than she'd ever suspected of such a big man, Colt guided his mom down the stairs. As Doris stepped into the first set of waiting arms, he threw a glance over his shoulder.

Was that gratitude shining in his eyes? Or interest? Emma swallowed. One meant she had some hope of succeeding on the Circle P. The other only spelled trouble.

Averting her eyes, she watched Garrett slip behind the wheel. Everyone waved their final goodbyes, and two vehicles headed for the highway. Soon after, more doors slammed and engines started. The caravan of pickup trucks and cars headed down the long driveway, their headlights cutting through the wisps of early morning fog.

Colt stood at the edge of the lawn, watching, until the procession curved around the trees and moved out of sight. As he turned to the ranch hands who'd joined the neighbors, all traces of the tenderness he'd shown minutes earlier disappeared.

"All right, let's get this day in gear. We're a man short without Josh, so there's no time to waste. I want the stalls mucked out before breakfast, the horses saddled and ready to ride. I saw some worn leather in the tack room. Somebody needs to get on that pronto. And don't forget to look for loose wire wherever you go. If I have to call the vet again, it's comin' out of your paychecks."

Clearly, Colt had buried the easygoing personality of the man who'd entertained his family the night before under a gruff exterior. Surprised by the sudden change and certain his next step would involve her own string of orders, Emma slipped through the front door, headed for the kitchen, where Tim and Chris sat at the table nursing cups of coffee.

"Mornin', ma'am." Tim swilled the last of his coffee and gulped it down. He jumped to his feet. "Mr. Colt told us to help you today. What's first?"

Before heading upstairs last night, she'd assembled the makings for a breakfast casserole. "I'll work on that," she told Tim while she buttoned her chef's jacket. "You chop green peppers and onions for the home fries." Ignoring his look of consternation, she put Chris to work carving strawberry flowers for a fruit bowl. When he balked, she took the knife from his hand.

"It's not enough that food tastes good," she explained, demonstrating. "It has to look appetizing. It's all part of the experience." She sprinkled kiwi stars across the melon and cantaloupe. "See?"

She took Chris's noncommittal shrug as a sign of progress. "Once you finish here, make sure everything else we need is on the serving counter. Salt, pepper, butter, jelly. Whatever the men want."

"Ketchup." Chris grinned. "And hot sauce."

Emma wrinkled her nose at the thought of either atop the tasty blend of eggs, cheese and sausage. Reading the truth in Chris's dark eyes, she shrugged. "Whatever they need."

The next hour passed in a blur of activity. A shiver of nervous energy passed through Emma while she put the finishing touches on breakfast. She told herself she had nothing to worry about. She'd certainly proven her abilities with far more complicated meals. She gave the array a final glance, straightened the edge of a dish and rang the bell. Not thirty seconds passed before the screened door opened and the first of the ranch hands wandered in. He hung his hat on one of the pegs at the entrance, grabbed a plate and served himself without ceremony. When he reached the potatoes, though, he hesitated.

"Can I get you anything else?" Recognizing the look of a dissatisfied customer, Emma braced herself.

The young cowboy glanced toward the door. "No, ma'am. Reckon not." With a shrug, he spooned potatoes onto his plate, leaving Emma to wonder what she'd done wrong. And what Colt would have to say about it.

COLT STEPPED INTO the kitchen as the last of the men took their places at the trestle table. *His men.* He squared his shoulders and told himself he'd best get used to carrying the added weight of responsibility. Until he turned the ranch over to the twins, the success or failure of the Circle P was in his hands. Every decision he made— from the bills he paid to whether or not he ordered the cattle moved to a new pasture—would affect the bottom line and thus the future of the land so many people depended on for their livelihood.

One look at the faces around the table told him he was about to encounter his first crisis of the day. Oh, the men were eating. He'd give them that. But the banter and easy jibes that usually accompanied meals in the kitchen were missing. He surveyed the counter where a bit of egg stuck to the sides of a nearly empty pan. Barely enough potatoes to make a mouthful dotted a serving platter. Two lonely biscuits sat on the edge of a plate.

"I see you waited for me," he said to no one in particular.

He'd meant it as a joke, but no one laughed. In fact, if the stricken look on some of the younger hands' faces was anything to go by, he'd only succeeded in pointing out the obvious. There wasn't enough food to go around. In silence, he scraped the dregs of the casserole onto his dish. He held the serving spoon over the fried potatoes. He had to do right by his men. Despite a growing sweet spot for the new cook, he pinned her with a pointed look.

"Where's the grits?"

"The what?" She folded her hands at the hem of her white jacket.

Abandoning his plate, Colt strode toward the pantry. He emerged seconds later with a five-pound bag cupped in one hand. "Grits." He plunked the bag on the counter. "They go good with eggs."

A frown crossed Emma's pretty little forehead. "Your mom never mentioned them."

"No need," Colt shot back. Every Southerner learned to cook ground corn shortly after they learned how to boil water. "Even I can make a passable bowl."

Emma unwound the twist tie and peered inside. "Rougher than cream of wheat," she murmured. She ran a finger through the granules. "Looks like polenta."

"Call it whatever you want. Just fix 'em for breakfast whenever there's eggs."

He moved to the rest of the meal. "There's onions and peppers in the potatoes," he announced as if no one else had made the discovery. He turned to face the cook. "What's that all about?" He took her noncommittal shrug for an evasive answer. "On the Circle P, we don't fancy up the hash browns with vegetables best saved for dinner."

"I'll make a note of that," she conceded. "No onions or peppers."

He lifted one of the remaining biscuits. "At least these are the same as Mom's." He broke it open and smeared it with jelly.

He wasn't sure why that last remark put a Cheshire cat smile on Emma's face. He decided he didn't care. Having said his piece, he scarfed down his breakfast while the others grabbed lunch bags and headed out the door. He waited till the last of them was out of earshot before he addressed the biggest problem.

"Emma, breakfast was a bit light. These are working men. Not guys in business suits who sit around the office. Stomachs are gonna rumble by lunchtime."

She surveyed the empty platters. Not even a scrap of food was left. She swallowed, nodding. "You think if I made twice as much?"

"Yeah, maybe. And some flapjacks."

"Pancakes, potatoes, biscuits *and* grits?"

When her brown eyes widened, he decided he liked the look and wanted to see it more often. He flexed his arm. "What can I say? Ranchin' is hard work."

That last comment earned him a laugh. Shaking her head, she sauntered toward the coffeepot.

He wouldn't mind getting used to the view, he supposed, though he didn't expect her to catch him taking a peek while she poured herself a cup. She tilted her head to the side and managed to look down her nose at him despite her petite stature. He grinned and shot her a glance that was all guilty pleasure while he showed her his palms.

The move darkened her eyes with an altogether different emotion. Answering her with a searing look of his own, he stepped closer.

"You have a smudge of something on your chin," he whispered, running a finger over her smooth cheek. Suddenly, the prospect of spending time with the new cook didn't seem like such an imposition. "I promised you a tour of the ranch. Will you have time today?" He could practically feel his arm wrapped around her waist while they covered the Circle P from one end to the other.

Her unwavering gaze scoured his face. "Bree will love it," she said slowly. "Give me an hour to get dinner preparations underway and we're all yours."

Colt set his rapidly cooling mug on the counter. Emma and Bree were a package deal, a fact it would do him well to remember. "I'll saddle the horses."

"I don't know." Emma turned pensive. "Neither of us has ever ridden."

He shrugged. "We'll take the Rhino, then." The four-seater wasn't the best way to see the ranch, but only a fool would take two inexperienced riders across the rough terrain on horseback. "It won't take as long, and I need to be back early enough to tackle bills and invoices this afternoon," he hedged, suddenly remembering he'd sworn not to fall behind on a never-ending, thankless task. He wiped his brow and headed for the door. "I'll be outside for a while."

Crossing to the barn, Colt grabbed a pitchfork. Glad for the manual labor that kept his fingers from wandering along soft cheeks, he began mucking out stalls. When the boys he'd assigned to the task put in an appearance, he paused for a moment to reevaluate. Nope, he decided. The woman had gotten under his skin, and there didn't seem to be anything he could do about it except suffer through their time together as best he could.

"Ya'll go find something else to do," he told the ranch hands, whose faces mirrored his own confusion.

Chapter Seven

"Mommy, I'm bored with coloring." Bree abandoned the scattered crayons on the kitchen table. "I want to do what you're doing." On tiptoe, she peered over the countertop.

Emma studied the preparations for tonight's dinner. Ready for the oven, six trussed hens—two more than she'd originally planned—waited in the refrigerator. Near the stove, vegetables simmered in immense Crock-Pots. Only a few carrots remained to be chopped for the salad—definitely not a job for little hands.

"Hang on, Bree. I'm almost done." She made smooth work of the thin slices.

Insistent hands tugged on the hem of her chef's whites. "Now, Mommy. Let me."

Emma stifled a groan. She had to prove she was up to the challenge of catering to the Circle P's workers and guests. And she had to do it quickly. Her first day on the job had gotten off to a rough start, and a crabby four-year-old wasn't going to make things any easier. Especially not when she felt just as off-balance and out of sorts as her daughter. But unlike Bree, she couldn't blame her irritability on a late night.

No, her cause had a handsome face and a name to go with it.

Colt Judd.

This morning's unexpected—and far too physical—run-in with the man in the darkened hallway had jolted her senses. Hours later, her chest still burned where she'd brushed against his solid muscles. Heat from his fingers lingered on her skin. Worse, once fired, her libido refused to calm down. She needed it to. Even if she wanted an attraction to the big, burly rancher—which she most certainly did not—she could give a dozen reasons why starting anything with Colt fell somewhere between bad idea and disaster.

Despite a softer side, the man was bossy, demanding. She could go on, but why bother? None of it mattered. Because his stay on the Circle P wasn't permanent. In less than a year, he'd return to his old life, his old job. Which didn't mesh at all with her plans to provide stability, permanence—a home—for her daughter.

"Let's go outside, Mommy." Bree raced to the door, where she rattled the handle.

"Maybe in a little bit." She couldn't blame her little girl for wanting to go. Except for yesterday's brief and nearly disastrous foray into the yard, they'd been cooped up inside ever since they arrived at the Circle P. "Mr. Colt said he'd take us for a tour of the ranch."

"That was a long, long time ago."

With a glance at the clock, Emma lowered the paring knife to the counter. In the three hours since she'd last seen him, Colt hadn't called, hadn't sent word. She slipped the salad into the refrigerator.

"You know, you're right." Hanging her white jacket on a nearby hook, she gave Bree a conspiratorial grin. "I think we should go exploring ourselves."

A little fresh air and sunshine would do them both some good. Bree would burn off some pent-up energy.

As for herself, well, a walk would probably cool her down. Enough that, when Colt finally did show up, she could make it through the afternoon without doing something truly stupid.

Like kissing the man.

She traced one finger across her lips. Yeah, *that* had bad idea written all over it.

"C'mon, Bree. There's a pond. We might see some fish. Or ducks. Want to check it out with me?" She slid leftover bread into a plastic bag, and held a hand out to her daughter. "Let's leave Mrs. Wickles here," she cautioned when Bree grabbed the doll. "You can tell her all about it when we get back."

On the way out the door, Emma tasked Tim with keeping an eye on the kitchen.

The young man frowned. "I got a bad feeling, Ms. Emma. Mr. Colt, he won't like it. You should wait for him."

"Then he should have shown up when he said he would." It wasn't as if she'd decided to go for a midnight run in Central Park. This was Florida, the land of sunny beaches and orange trees. Standing at the door, she shielded her eyes. Cattle grazed far beyond a fence on the other side of the pond. "We're not even going as far as the pasture. In fact, we'll stay within sight of the house."

She waved to her helper. She'd already sprayed Bree with sunblock, and her daughter raced ahead, eager for adventure. At the edge of the lawn, a clear path led through the knee-high grass toward glistening water. While Bree stopped to admire every bug that crossed their path, Emma took in a view far different from the sliver of light that had filtered through the grimy window in their New York apartment. Here, green was the color of the day. Tiny buds topped the tall grass. Palm fronds that looked like giant fans made dry whispers in the light breeze.

Bree ran her finger along the edge of one and giggled.

Grass rustled. A bird with a red beak poked its head above the weeds practically in front of them. Giant wings flapping, it took flight.

Emma held her breath, waiting for her daughter's reaction, but Bree only laughed.

"He's funny!" She looked around, her eyes wide. "There's a lot of birds here."

Gray cranes posed on stiltlike limbs before prodding the grass with long beaks. White birds paraded around on long, skinny legs that looked too slender to support their round middles. High overhead, crows with enormous wingspans flew in lazy circles above the pond. Thinking of the owl she'd heard from the porch this morning, Emma pushed loose hair back from her face.

They watched a turtle make its slow way across the path, but when Bree wanted to take it back to the ranch with them, Emma put her foot down. "I'm sure he already has a home."

"Where?" Bree wanted to know. "What do turtles eat? Is that a baby turtle? Where's its momma and daddy?"

"All good questions," Emma said. "Tell you what. Next time we go into town, we'll stop at the library. I bet they have lots of books about the animals that live here. We'll learn all about them."

At the edge of the pond, lily pads dotted water the color of strong coffee. While cicadas filled the air with their raspy sounds and grass swayed, minnows flitted between the fat green leaves floating on the surface.

Bree delighted in watching the fish swim and spent five glorious minutes simply counting bubbles that rose from tiny mouths. When her interest waned, Emma handed her a slice of bread. Together, they crumbled pieces into the water and laughed as hundreds of minnows swam into the shallows.

Since Bree was still bursting with energy by the time they'd used up all the bread, they struck out on the path that skirted the pond. A pond that was actually more of a lake, Emma decided as the trail narrowed to a deeply rutted track. A thick branch floated near the shore. Emma caught Bree's arm, putting a quick end to her daughter's plan to walk across the makeshift bridge. No matter how shallow the water, the idea of her child going for a dip sent a shiver down her spine. Uneasy, she glanced over her shoulder at the treeless shoreline. A laugh bubbled up from her chest when she spotted the house and barn less than a hundred yards away.

"Look, Mommy! It's a nest. Like a bird's nest. Only it's on the ground." Bree started toward a pile of grass and debris. "Do you think the turtle lives there?"

Emma tugged on her bottom lip. "That's a pretty long walk for a s-l-o-w turtle," she said, drawing the words out.

Bree grabbed a nearby twig. "Let's look inside. Maybe there's babies."

Or snakes. Or... Emma shivered. "Not a good idea, honey." She took the stick from her daughter's hand. "How would you like it if someone came into your house and poked around?"

Deep gouges marred the mud surrounding the nest. What would make such large tracks? Emma studied them, the unease from a moment ago deepening to concern. Maybe coming out here hadn't been such a good plan after all, she decided as the idea that it was time to go back landed solidly in her chest. Looking up, she spotted Bree's dark curls a split second before her daughter disappeared behind tall grass at a curve in the path.

"Bree! Don't you dare take another step," Emma called. Rounding the corner, she slid to a halt.

Alligators.

Two of the largest she'd ever seen—actually the only ones she'd ever seen outside a zoo—lay sunning themselves on a muddy beach. Only feet away from them, Bree stood, her thumb in her mouth. The log they'd spotted earlier moved farther along the shore. Two eyes blinked open at one end of a long snout that *wasn't* made of wood.

Emma's heart leaped to her throat.

"Bree, baby," she whispered. "Don't move, honey."

She closed the distance between them on silent feet.

Easing her daughter into her arms, she prayed for a sturdy stick, a bush high enough to keep Bree out of harm's way, a tree to climb. Nada. She eyed the alligators, wondering how fast they could move. One of them opened a gaping jaw filled with immense, sharp teeth, and she froze.

Crap.

WITH ONE BLOW, Colt drove the loose nail into the board. Hammer in hand, he walked the perimeter of the stall, checking for protrusions or splinters that could pierce a horse's flesh, gouge a soft mouth, put out an eye. Satisfied he'd dispatched any dangers, he rattled the latch to make sure it hadn't worked loose. He eyed his handiwork, amused that such an insignificant accomplishment should fill him with more pride than hearing thousands cheer for him at the World Finals in Las Vegas.

Stepping from the enclosure, he rapped his knuckles on the top rail. No, sir, there was nothing quite like a few hours of honest, hard work to clear the mind. This morning, he'd worked his way through a half dozen stalls, shoveling manure and spreading fresh straw. By the time he finished with the rest of the barn, he figured to rid himself of all thoughts of a certain petite, dark-haired newcomer.

"Mr. Colt?" A lean figure crossed the strip of bright sunlight that shone through the wide opening at the end of the aisle.

"Back here," he called.

Boots sounded against the floor. "Hank said to tell you he got bumped off his flight. He's taking the next one out and won't get to Tallahassee before late tonight."

"You made it back already?" Colt propped his hands atop the pitchfork. The trip from the Circle P to West Palm and back should have taken Josh at least four hours. He stole a peek at his watch.

Great.

He'd lost track of the time. If he didn't get a move on, he'd run out of daylight before he finished touring the ranch with Emma and Bree.

And there it was.

The restless feeling he'd spent hours banishing rushed over him again.

"Since you're back, how 'bout finishing up here?" He leaned the pitchfork toward Josh while he stripped off a pair of soiled work gloves. "Leave the last stall on the right. Maize's in there." One of a dozen or so cattle dogs had made the spot her home till she weaned her new pups.

"Yes, sir, boss." Josh hefted the tool on his way past.

Several long strides took Colt into stifling, midday heat. Despite the cooler temperatures in the barn, he wondered if a shower might be in order before he stepped foot in the kitchen. He shook his head. Getting all spiffed up wasn't going to help squelch his attraction to the petite brunette. It would only make things worse. Instead, he detoured to the big porcelain trough outside the barn only long enough to wash the worst of the grime from his hands and arms before he followed the walkway around to the back of the house.

"Sorry I'm late." He sniffed and drank in a lungful of appetizing scents, but instead of the cook, Tim stood at the stove. Colt let his smile fade. "Have you seen Emma and Bree?" he asked.

"They're gone, Mr. Colt."

"Gone? Gone where?" He pictured the duo on the road to faraway places, out of his life completely. An empty feeling he didn't expect and wasn't at all prepared for filled his chest.

"Ms. Emma, she took the little girl for a walk." The scent of rich chocolate rose from the oven when Tim held the door ajar. "She took bread for the fish," he added after slipping his hands into oven mitts.

The uneasy feeling Colt had been fighting made a nauseating plunge into his stomach. He grabbed the counter to keep himself upright. His voice roughened. "And you let them go?"

The pans Tim had been holding rattled onto the counter. He retreated a step, his hands outstretched. "Ms. Doris went to the pond. Plenty of times."

"She knew what to look out for," Colt growled. "Emma doesn't."

Spiders. Scorpions. Snakes. He started with the small things. Thinking of Emma and Bree facing down a few of the larger predators that roamed the Circle P wouldn't help the situation. Not at all. No, those thoughts would only drive him insane.

He registered a sharp pop as the door slapped against its frame behind him. He veered toward the barn, but straightened. By the time he grabbed a horse and saddled up, any number of bad things could have happened. Even now, he could be too late. He broke into a run. But no matter how quickly he moved, he couldn't get past the feeling he wasn't going fast enough.

Seconds that felt like hours passed before he spotted Emma standing clear across the pond. One look, and he knew he'd been right to worry. Trouble had found her. He scanned the tall grass. At first, he didn't see Bree and his stomach ratcheted tighter. He sucked in a gulp of air when a light breeze whispered across the open plain. The grass parted, revealing the little girl clinging to her mother's side.

Neither moved a muscle.

Snakes. Gators. Panthers. Boar. All manner of wildlife roamed the area around the Everglades. Colt flexed his fingers and wished he'd stopped long enough to pick up a rifle. Without it, he eyed the water that stretched between him and the spot where Emma stood. Only someone with a death wish swam in an alligator hole, and he didn't want anyone to die today. Instead, he hit the deer trail that ran along the shore.

Though his mind screamed at him to go faster, he slowed the second he spotted the nest. Staring at the telltale imprint of a large tail in the dried mud, he suppressed a shudder. The scar on his leg throbbed, a reminder of what could happen if someone got between a mama gator and her eggs. He wrenched his thoughts away from images of snapping jaws, weeks of bandages and painful rehabilitation. So far, Emma and Bree were okay. It was his job to see they stayed that way.

He stopped at the edge of the grass, both to assess the situation and to catch his breath. His heart sank as he studied the two twelve-footers that lay on the bank, their mouths agape. From the water, a third set of eyes stared intently toward the shore. Judging the distance from the gators to the spot where Emma had frozen, and from there to where he stood, Colt swallowed a curse.

"Emma," he called softly. "I'm gonna get you out of this."

"Co-olt."

Her panic-tinged voice plunged a knife into his chest. "Just stay right where you are," he ordered. Wishing like heck he could follow the same advice, he edged into the clearing. "Nine times out of ten, a gator'll head straight for the water," he said, keeping his voice low and even despite his hammering heart.

Though he hadn't lied, it was that tenth time that had tied his stomach in knots. Cold-blooded or not, mama gators could get a mite testy when it came to protecting their young. With her nest not a dozen yards behind him, the odds weren't good that this one or her mate would turn tail and run. The big reptiles moved fast when they wanted.

Without taking his eyes off the animals, he sidled up to Emma. "I'll take Bree." He reached for the little girl, who clung to her mother. He let his voice drop into the same tone his dad had used when he'd been young and stupid and gotten himself in trouble. "We're gonna play a game, but you have to let me hold you." He pried tiny fingers loose and whisked Bree onto his shoulders.

Off to his left, something crackled through the underbrush. *Time to get moving.*

Pitching his voice below the range of little ears, he whispered, "Okay. So here's what we're gonna do. Slowly. Very. Slowly. We're going to back ourselves out of here. That big male—" he aimed his chin toward the smaller gator "—he'll probably ignore us. The one in the water'll stay put. It's the female we need to worry about. If she charges, run. Fast as you can. Straight down the trail. Don't stop. Not till you're well past her nest. You got that?"

Though her brown eyes widened, Emma nodded.

"So here we go." Watching to make sure they moved together, he took a careful step. "So far, so good," Colt hissed.

They made it halfway out of the clearing before Emma's foot landed on a twig.

Crack!

With a blur of churning legs, the smaller of the two alligators slid into the water. The other one did a one-eighty so fast it made Colt's head spin. Looking even larger and more menacing on its feet, the animal stood its ground. A threatening hiss vibrated in the still air. The noise sent a shiver down Colt's spine.

"She's gonna charge. I'll distract her while you make a run for it."

The panic in Emma's eyes deepened into downright terror.

"Don't worry," he soothed. "Bree and I will be right

behind you." Deftly he swept his hat from his head. "Ready. Set. Run!"

Holding the Stetson by its brim, he flung it, Frisbee-style, past the animal's nose. Feet flying, jaws snapping, the gator struck the hat while Emma moved at warp speed in the opposite direction. Matching her stride for stride, Colt caught up with her when they were halfway to the house.

One run-in with the local wildlife exceeded his daily limit, and he glanced around, making sure no other varmints lingered nearby. When he was sure they were safe, he slid Bree into her mother's arms. Emma cradled the little girl's head to her chest while Colt took a deep breath.

"In Florida, anywhere there's a mudhole, you're gonna have gators. You gotta watch out for things like that."

The informative tone he'd aimed for must have missed its mark because, pale as a fresh T-shirt, Emma pinned him with narrowed brown eyes.

"Too bad no one mentioned it. That might have been nice to know, you know, *before* we left the house."

A warmth that had nothing to do with exertion or heat flooded his face. Educating her, that was also his job. A job he'd failed to do.

"You're right. I was late. I got…" What could he say? Certainly not that he'd worked in the barn all morning in order to banish her from his thoughts. He let out a slow, unsteady breath. "…tied up."

Emma brushed a hand through her daughter's tangled hair. "You okay, baby?"

"Mommy, you're holding me too tight." Bree pulled

away, peeking up at him from her mother's arms. "I liked riding on you. We went fast!"

"Want to do it again?" At Bree's vigorous nod, Colt reached for the child. But when his fingers brushed against Emma, his stomach sank. The woman who'd seemed so brave, so trusting, shook like a palsied calf.

The minute he settled her daughter onto his shoulders, Colt drew the petite brunette to him, surprised when she practically stumbled into his arms. An urge to keep her there forever surged through him as her head landed on his chest. He cupped her ice-cold fingers in his warm ones.

"Mr. Colt, we fed the fish," Bree prattled from her perch. "We saw a turtle and a great big turtle's nest. I wanted to see the baby turtles, but Mommy said no. We saw birds. Mommy called one bird a crane, but that's silly. Cranes build buildings. Where we used to live, we saw lots of them."

"I'm sorry," Colt whispered into Emma's hair. "My fault. This was all my fault."

He hung on, determined not to let her go until her legs stopped quaking. For long seconds, they clung to one another while Bree chirped overhead. At last, he felt Emma's chest expand. She stirred, the movement triggering a sudden awareness of slim hips pressed against his thighs, his arm around a trim waist, firm breasts against his...

He released her and stepped back.

What had he been thinking? *Nothing,* he told himself. He hadn't been thinking about anything. Certainly not white picket fences or the kind of roots that didn't figure into his life on the road. No, he was only doing what he was supposed to do—keeping Emma and Bree safe. Nothing more. Nothing less. But despite his stern lecture, he threaded his fingers through Emma's. Her hand in his, he led the way toward the house.

"Hey, Little Bit," he called to the child who sat, lighter than a feed sack, on his shoulders. "How's the view up there?"

"Good!" Bree leaned back, her viselike hold on his forehead tightening. "I can see the whole world from here."

Colt clamped a steadying hand on the little girl's bottom. "I'll show you more stuff this afternoon when we go for a ride around the rest of the ranch."

"We might have to wait on that." Emma searched his face, the odd expression on her own letting him know he'd missed something. "I think we've had enough excitement for one day, don't you?"

Though spending more time with Emma and Bree was exactly what he wanted to do, Colt shoved his disappointment way down deep where it wouldn't show. There'd be other times, other chances, he reminded himself. He even managed a casual, "Yep, I reckon you're right."

Minutes later, he stood, watching mother and daughter walk into the house without him. He told himself he ought to be glad Emma had canceled their tour for the afternoon. Especially since it gave him time to accomplish a few other things on his agenda. Like taking a shower. He could muck stalls and fight alligators without breaking a sweat, but put him within five feet of the feisty little cook, and a shower moved to the top of his list.

A cold one.

Chapter Eight

Emma squinted at the clock on the nightstand. Two in the morning. She flipped over onto her back and stretched one arm above her head. When alligators still prowled the backs of her eyelids, she admitted defeat. No matter how many cute, fluffy sheep gaily jumping over fences she counted, she'd never be able to relax as long as every one of them landed in a puddle of snapping jaws and swishing tails.

She eased herself out of bed. Careful not to disturb the child sprawled across the mattress, she tucked the covers beneath a tiny chin and pressed a kiss against her daughter's cheek. Bree didn't so much as stir.

"Thank goodness," she whispered. She had Colt to thank for the child's peaceful sleep. The man had turned their brush with danger into an adventure for her four-year-old. Over dinner, he'd shown even more of his protective side when he'd impressed his men with a lecture on watching out for all their guests, including her daughter. Especially her daughter.

A slow sigh escaped Emma's lips. The man was full of surprises, not the least of which was the moment she'd spent in his arms. She could still feel his hands at her waist. Still hear the steady thudding of his heart. Hours later, she caught his faint scent whenever she ran a hand through her hair. None of which helped her relax. Quite the opposite, it stirred an odd restlessness within her.

Tugging a sweatshirt over her pajamas, she headed downstairs for the one tried-and-true method of calming her nerves. In the pantry, she gathered ingredients for one of her favorite recipes. She set to work, confident her activities wouldn't disturb Bree. As for Colt, well, the rancher's temporary quarters were on the far side of the house. She doubted the noise she made in the kitchen would reach him, though it took more effort than she liked to resist a quick peek in on him to double-check.

Soon, the makings for a special cake littered the counter. Dense and dark, with a rich peanut butter filling, the dessert would make the perfect thank-you gift for the man who had rapidly made a habit of saving her daughter's life. Only, she had a sneaking suspicion that Colt Judd, with his brilliant blue eyes and easy swagger, was even more dangerous than wild animals.

The man was an enigma. At once cold and hot, fierce and tender. She wished she knew what lay beneath his brusque exterior. At his core, was he like her dad, her first husband? Or did he have a compassionate heart? Uncertainty gnawed at her as she beat together flour and sugar, eggs and cocoa. Colt could have read her the riot act this afternoon. Yet, he hadn't. She couldn't forget how he'd whispered into her ear, practically begged for her forgiveness. His kindness stirred a longing she thought she'd securely locked away, if not forever, then at least until she and Bree had a home of their own.

The only thing that hadn't wavered about the man was his insistence on preserving the very traditions she threatened with the changes she wanted to make, the things she didn't know and, worst of all, the ones she'd ruined. So even if spending time with the tall, handsome rancher sent her heart into overdrive, the best thing, the smartest thing, she could do for both of them was to stay as far away from him as possible.

Tension bled from her shoulders as she reached her decision. She shoved aside a wish that things could be different and lost herself in the task at hand. Later, padding into the living room while the cakes cooled, she paused at the sound of ice clinking against the sides of a glass. Squinting, she peered into the darkness. Her heart stuttered when she traced the outline of a figure on the sofa. She skimmed over the shape of a familiar head, traveled the wide shoulders down to muscular arms.

Colt. The man she'd decided to stay away from sat on the leather couch, his feet propped on the coffee table. Overcoming an urge to retreat into the kitchen, she forced herself across the room.

"I didn't wake you, did I?" she asked when she neared him.

"Nah." His deep voice rose from the darkness. "Couldn't sleep. You?"

Regretting that she hadn't slipped into something decidedly *less* comfortable than thin pajamas and a blousy sweatshirt, she remained glued to the floor. "I couldn't get this afternoon out of my mind. What could have happened—what would have happened—if you hadn't shown up when you did."

"Aw, it wasn't as bad as it looked." He patted the empty cushion beside him. "Come. Sit a spell."

Though a voice in her head argued that spending any time alone with Colt wasn't the best idea, she shushed it. She slid onto the sofa with a newfound determination to learn more about the man who had her emotions in such a quandary. The soft cushion bowed beneath her, tipping her close enough to feel the warmth that emanated from him.

"Most of the time, gators are more afraid of us than we are of them."

Emma hugged herself. "You could have fooled me."

"Yeah, about that. They're also very protective of their young. If it hadn't been for the nest, the ones today would've swum off the minute you stepped onto their beach. But getting between an alligator and its eggs or hatchlings—yeah, you don't want to do that."

"When that one opened his mouth..." Her voice trailed off. She licked her lips and tried again. "All those teeth. I thought for sure it wanted to eat us." She was so lost in the terror of those few moments that she didn't object when Colt slid an arm around her shoulders. His solid strength felt natural and protective, and she leaned closer.

"Nah," he said with a shrug. "They're cold-blooded. They open their jaws wide like that, particularly when it's hot out. It helps 'em regulate their body temperature. Looks scary as hell, but they don't mean anything by it. Gotta stay out of the water, though. They're not the smartest animals in the kingdom. They've been known to mistake a swimmer for a fish."

He sat so close she knew the moment his muscles tensed. She studied the hand he kneaded against one thigh.

"Tell me none of them ever got hold of you," she whispered, unable to fathom how anyone would survive a run-in with the huge creatures. She gasped when he nodded.

"I was eight." The heady scent of good whiskey

swirled through the air as he reached for his glass. He took a long pull before he continued. "I was lucky. The one that grabbed me wasn't much bigger than I was. Plus, Ty and Garrett were there. They pulled him off of me. Or me outta him—it all happened so fast, the details never were real clear. Forty-two stitches right across here." He pointed to his leg. "After that, I made it a point to learn all I could about gators, though I can't say they're my favorite critters."

Emma inhaled sharply. What if she hadn't stopped Bree from wading into the water? What would have happened then? Though she tightened her arms about herself, a series of tremors turned her insides to jelly.

"Hey. C'mere." Colt's fingers drew her closer. "You don't have to worry. They're gone now."

"I know." A mud-splattered truck filled with long cages had rattled past the kitchen window shortly after supper. The sun had long since set by the time she heard it return. Only this time, a heavy load pressed the truck's back end so low it almost scraped the tires. "It's just…" She paused while she fought down another tremor.

Colt's hand gave her shoulders a squeeze. "We've never lost an employee or a guest on the Circle P. I'm not about to break with tradition on my watch."

Tradition. Colt's favorite word.

"So what will happen to them, the alligators?" Straightening slightly, Emma steered the conversation to something that didn't stir thoughts of turning toward Colt and wrapping her arms around his wide chest.

"The trapper'll sell the eggs or hatchlings to an alligator farm. The adults, well, it depends. He might harvest the meat and skins. Or release them in the Everglades where they won't bother anybody."

Despite telling herself it was a bad idea, Emma leaned toward Colt. "So if we're safe, why are both of us wide awake at—" she checked her watch "—three in the morning."

"Me, my mind won't let go." He swirled ice cubes and took another pull from his drink. "Running the ranch is a big job. I'm not sure I realized how big when I took it on." Setting his glass on the side table, he flexed his fingers. "Don't know how my dad did it. I sure don't want to let him down."

This vulnerable side of Colt was rapidly undoing her first impression of the man. A desire to know more about his past stirred within her. "You sure know your way around this place." She tipped her hand, indicating the rest of the ranch. "How long have you been away?"

"I lived here till I earned my card in the PBR—that's Professional Bull Riders—when I turned eighteen."

"You were in the rodeo?" She imagined him sitting astride an animal the size of Three while a stadium filled with people cheered for him. "Why?"

"You've never been to a rodeo, have you?"

Hearing the note of disbelief in Colt's voice, she shook her head.

"I'll have to take you sometime. There's nothing quite like it. Whether you rope steers or barrel race, you're constantly testing yourself against your limits. Trying to beat the clock. You want to ride longer, hold on tighter than the time before. Bull riding was my specialty. I was pretty good at it. Won a couple of national championships."

Emma leaned back. Colt sounded an awful lot like her dad talking about the military. "And that's the job you'll go back to after you leave here?"

"Nah." He shook his head. "I retired from the circuit years ago."

"Retired?" The concept was so foreign, she gaped up at him. "At what? Thirty?" She didn't have to see Colt's face to know a grin had spread across it.

"Just shy of it. Rodeoing is hard enough on the body that hardly anyone competes much past their twenties. I've had my share of cracked ribs, sprains and bruises. Only had one really bad spill—that one sidelined me for three months. It was worth it, though. Mom has my gold buckles stashed around here somewhere."

Emma blinked. He'd endured all kinds of injuries for a belt buckle? She shook her head. There had to be more to it than that. "So what's a retired bull rider do?"

"Pretty much the same thing…without the bulls. I travel ahead of the riders and the riggers. Work with the livestock contractors. Oversee the vendors. Make sure we comply with all the safety regs. Abilene one week. Kansas City the next. I show up, do my job and move on."

"But you gave all that up. To come back here?"

"This is home," he said as if that explained everything. "At least, it is till Royce and Randy finish up their contract around the first of the year. Once they get here, I'll go back to the PBR."

She couldn't ignore the cool wave of disappointment that rushed over her when she considered never seeing Colt again. But his stay on the Circle P was only a temporary stop in a life on the move.

"Sounds like we're exact opposites," she murmured. Immediately, she caught the wistful note in her voice and wished it away. But it was too late. Colt had heard it, too. He leaned close enough that his breath brushed her cheek.

"How so?"

She really had no choice but to tell him the truth. "Between growing up as an army brat and my marriage to Jack, I've moved so many times, I've lost count."

"Jack, he's your husband?"

"Was. Our marriage didn't last. Honestly, I was surprised we made it as long as we did. We were supposed to go to school, open a restaurant together. I'd cook. He'd handle the front of the house. We'd become so famous they'd do a TV show about us. Then…" She poked a spot on her shirt. "Then my dad talked him into joining the army. He convinced Jack it was a great way to earn an education. Only thing was, Jack loved the military. He was always ready for the next challenge, the next set of orders. Me, not so much."

"It took a lot of guts, starting out on your own."

"I had Bree." Emma smiled. "She's the reason I finally called it quits. I wanted something better for my daughter. Wanted her to have the stability, the roots, I never had. To grow up in a household where people respected one another. I'd just filed for divorce when Jack died in a—" she made air quotes "—routine training accident."

"I knew you were a widow. But I had no idea. Bree must have been just a baby."

"It's been four years." Four long, tough years. She scrubbed a palm along the seam of her pajamas. "Jack's life insurance paid my way through culinary school. I got a job in New York. Worked my way up to sous chef, or second in line. I still had my eyes on fame and fortune.

But then I realized all the accolades in the world weren't worth what I'd have to endure to get them."

"And here you are."

"Yeah. Here I am. It took a couple of years to figure out that working in New York was just more of the same atmosphere I was trying to get away from. My last boss had a legendary temper. So when your mom and dad offered me a position on the Circle P, I jumped at the chance. To me it meant not just peace and quiet, but stability and home." But life had an odd way of throwing monkey wrenches into her plans. She certainly hadn't intended to dunk the Circle P's cookbook in a watery bath. Any more than she'd planned on an attraction to a certain tall, dark and handsome rancher.

"You're looking for adventure," she finished, as much for herself as for Colt. "I want to settle down."

"Sounds like we're headed in different directions."

"I'm afraid so."

She expected Colt to pull away. Thought that, despite the moment they'd shared this afternoon, he'd come to the same realization that they were wrong for one another. When he didn't move, she decided she'd have to be the one to leave. To march into the kitchen, where she'd put the finishing touches on the cake she'd started. It was what any smart, sane person would do.

Unfortunately, smart wasn't exactly how she felt sitting next to Colt in the middle of the night in a house where the only other living being was a four-year-old sound asleep upstairs. Hungry, maybe. And not for the dessert she'd started when thoughts of alligators had kept her awake. Colt's touch stirred a visceral response, one that had everything to do with wanting the big rancher's arms around hers, his lips pressed against hers.

Smart went out the window when he feathered soft kisses across her forehead. She drew in a breathy sigh and tipped her face to his. Instantly, he covered her mouth with his own. The press of his lips against hers sent tingles racing along every nerve in her body. With the first brush of his tongue against her lips, she opened to him. He tasted of excellent single malt mingled with mint. Beneath the crisp, clean smells of fresh air and soap, she caught a hint of his own musky scent. His fingers cupped her face. His thumb traced the tender skin beneath her jaw.

Her breath caught in her throat and she gave herself to the heady sensations of Colt's touch, his taste. She moaned her pleasure, refusing to listen to the voice of reason that practically shouted that kissing Colt Judd was a bad idea. A very bad idea.

One thing for sure, she thought when they both finally came up for air, Colt had succeeded in erasing all thoughts of four-legged predators from her mind. Except a new worry had taken its place and, she feared that, unlike the cold-blooded kind, this one wouldn't let go.

BREE'S FEET SKIDDED to a halt halfway to the barn. She turned, clutching Mrs. Wickles to her chest. "Are we gonna see horses?"

Colt eyed the girl's mom. Usually attentive to her daughter's every need, Emma studied the distant horizon without answering. Was she thinking about their kiss? Did she regret it? He scuffed a boot through the dust. He could think of dozens of reasons they should stay at arm's length. She was his employee. He, her boss. She wanted to put down roots. He lived a rootless existence.

All things considered, common sense told him he should maintain a healthy distance from the cook.

Except fate kept throwing them together. Fate, and a little girl who needed rescuing far too often. Then there was the little matter of last night. Or, more precisely, this morning. How was he to know a restless night would land them in each other's arms? That her kisses would have knocked his boots off if he'd been wearing them. Her touch was so tempting he wished he hadn't promised to take Emma and her daughter on a tour of the ranch. Or to spend his evenings helping her re-create the Circle P's traditional recipes. How he was going to manage either of those tasks without slipping his arm around Emma's slim waist, or stealing a kiss from her perfect lips, he had no idea.

He looked down at the little girl who danced around on her toes. At least they had Bree along with them this afternoon. The pint-size chaperone would keep things from getting too heated.

"Just Star and Daisy," he said, answering her question. "I bet they'd like some company."

"Horses, Mommy!" Bree's head bobbed up and down so fast, she sent her pigtails flying. She tugged on her mom's hand. "I'm gonna ride one all by myself!"

The boast earned Emma's full attention. "Horses are not toys," she warned. "We have to be careful around them. Listen to Mr. Colt and do exactly what he says."

Knowing Emma trusted him with her daughter sent warmth spreading across his chest. He treated them both to his best teasing grin. "She's got a bit of daredevil in her, doesn't she?" He pulled one of Bree's ponytails. "Are you sure you're not a tomboy?"

Both of Bree's little hands landed on her hips. "You're silly, Mr. Colt. I'm a girl."

"Bree, mind your manners." The glint of humor in Emma's eyes softened her stern words.

"It's okay." Colt laughed. "I *was* being silly." He reached for his hat brim and was momentarily thrown off-balance when his fingers encountered nothing but air. Playing Frisbee with a full-size alligator was mighty hard on a cowboy hat. Not that he was complaining. When he got right down to it, he didn't really mind that a few shreds of leather were all that was left of his best work Stetson. Not if it meant Bree and Emma were safe.

"How 'bout if I carry you." Colt didn't wait for an answer but swept the featherweight child into his arms. As he strode into the darkened barn, two long faces appeared over Dutch doors at the far end of the row. Star and Daisy nickered, hoping for a treat.

"Oooh!" Bree huddled against his neck. "They're big!"

"Yep," Colt agreed. To give both mom and daughter time to get used to the idea, he showed them the layout.

"Ty made a lot of changes once Jimmy and Sarah moved in." He pointed to the pitchforks, rakes and shovels that hung at shoulder height near the entrance. A ladder to the upper level collapsed into the ceiling. "It's meant to keep inquisitive youngsters from testing their wings from the hayloft." He winced remembering the day Hank had broken a leg when he missed landing on a pile of hay. He sure didn't want that happening to Bree.

"Saddles, bridles and riding gear are stored in here." Crossing to the tack room, he inhaled the familiar scent of leather when he opened the door on racks of neatly hung equipment. Cowboy hats of various sizes and colors hung on a peg wall. With Bree's help, he chose one that would do until he made a trip to Eli's Western Wear for a replacement. He grabbed a couple of carrots from a fifty-pound bag by the door. Leading the way, he headed down the wide, clear aisle to the horses' stalls.

"Want to give Daisy a treat?" Colt broke the vegetable into smaller pieces.

Worry lines crisscrossed Bree's little face. "Does she bite?" Looking for reassurance, she swung a hopeful look toward her mom.

Emma's lips parted as if she wanted to protest, but Colt intervened before she had a chance. "This old gal has the best manners of any horse on the Circle P." He held a carrot out to Bree.

Bree pursed a pair of rosebud lips, clearly torn between fear and daring. He grinned at Emma when her daughter finally gathered enough courage to say, "Okay."

"Here, hold your hand flat," he instructed. "She has big teeth, but her mouth is soft as velvet."

One arm curled tightly around Colt's neck, Bree held still while Daisy lipped the piece of carrot from her open palm.

"Mommy, she tickled me!" Light sparkled in Bree's eyes. "Can I give her another one?"

"That was really good, Bree." Colt gave the kid points for bravery. "You can pet her if you want. She'd like that."

Carefully, Bree reached out to the gentle mare. She ran a hand along the shiny coat and giggled when Daisy signaled her contentment by blowing air through soft lips.

Colt locked on Emma's eyes. The fear he'd glimpsed in them had turned to wonder. Her wordless *thank you* sent another wave of warmth through his chest. He took a deep breath. Staying away from the petite brunette was going to be harder than he'd ever imagined if something as simple as introducing her daughter to a horse put a glow in Emma's eyes.

But the moment passed when Bree turned up her nose. "She's pooping!" the little girl screamed in a mix of horror and delight.

"Yep," Colt chuckled. "Horses do that." He turned to Emma. "We muck the stalls twice a day, every day, replacing soiled hay with fresh bedding. Keeps the horses healthy." He nudged Bree's tummy. "And everything smells nice."

Figuring they'd spent enough time with the horses, he lifted one finger to his lips. "If you can be real quiet, we'll take a peek at Maize's puppies."

"Puppies!" Bree's eyes widened.

She scrambled to get down, but Colt had been around the four-year-old enough to hang on to her. "They're too small to handle," he cautioned. "We can only look. No touching."

The little girl gave him a solemn nod. With Emma at his side, they peered over the Dutch door at the end of the aisle. Maize sprawled across a bed of fresh hay and old horse blankets while three of her six pups nursed. Two of the others slept in a pile, one on top of the other. The runt of the litter nosed his way across the straw.

"Oh, Mommy, they're so cute." Bree wrapped one arm around Colt's neck. "Can I have a puppy? Please, please, please?"

Looking into the child's pleading eyes, Colt felt his heart lurch. He'd give her a puppy. Hell, she could have the whole litter if she wanted. He was on the verge of saying so, when Emma's voice reminded him the decision wasn't his to make.

"Bree, it's not nice to ask for presents."

"She's a good dog, with a kind heart," Colt chimed in. "Her pups'll likely take after her. Shouldn't every kid have responsibility for a dog?"

"Do not fall under her spell, Colt Judd," Emma admonished, though the amused expression on her face told him she was only half serious. "We'll have to wait and see. How long before they're weaned?"

"Another six weeks, give or take." At her quick nod, he turned to Bree. "Right now, the puppies' eyes are shut." Almost as if he'd timed it, the wandering pup bumped into the stable wall and fell in a heap. "They need to stay with their mom till they grow a bit. Let's let the pups go back to sleep for now."

When Bree shook her head and pouted, it nearly broke his heart, but a glance at Emma helped him stay firm. "We'll come back to see them again," he swore. "You have to promise me you won't come out here alone, though. Your mommy or me, we have to come with you."

Bree took a big, shuddery breath. "Okay, Mr. Colt," she agreed. She waved one hand at the dogs. "Bye-bye, puppies," she said in a sad little voice that ripped another hole in his heart.

Torn between standing at the door watching the pups for the rest of the day, and taking Emma on the promised tour of the ranch, Colt hesitated. He shot her a questioning glance. The knowing smile she wore told him he wasn't the first to fall prey to her daughter's charms. Unless he missed his guess, he wouldn't be the last.

Heaven help the boys, he thought, putting his feet in

motion. Behind the barn, he settled Bree and Mrs. Wickles in the backseat of a canvas-topped vehicle.

"Horseback's the best way to see the ranch, but we'll save that till after you and Bree have a few riding lessons under your belts." He wasn't much older than the little girl the first time he rode solo. As for Emma… For a moment he lost himself in the image of his hands at her hips as she climbed into the saddle for the first time.

"You leave the keys in the ignition?"

Emma's voice snagged his concentration, dragging it back to the present. He looked down. The keys for the Rhino dangled from his fingers.

"Who's gonna steal anything?" He shrugged. This was farm country, where neighbors looked out for each other. "Let me gas 'er up, and we'll get moving." He cranked the engine and drove the sturdy golf cart toward the tank at the edge of the building, where he used the little car's battery to jump-start the pump. With the tank topped off, he slid behind the wheel.

Space was tight in the four-seater. He eyed the trim legs that stretched from the hem of Emma's shorts to her sandals, where sparkly nail polish glittered on her toes. An urge to trace his fingers along her smooth skin nearly overwhelmed him, and he gulped, almost thankful for their backseat chaperone.

To give his hands something to do, he shoved the stick into gear. Bree let out a happy giggle when he eased the Rhino off the graveled path and onto a deeply rutted track that led away from the buildings. "Parkers have owned the Circle P for more than a hundred years," he said, raising his voice to be heard over the throaty engine. "Judds have managed the land for just as long. Round here, this is considered a small ranch, but Ty's been adding to the holdings. In a couple of years, we've gone from a thousand acres to twenty-five hundred. We lease another couple of sections. It takes a lot of land to feed cattle on grass and silage."

He pulled to a stop at a gate that stretched between two sections of fence. Hopping out, he unlatched a heavy chain and shoved the gate open. He slid behind the wheel again and drove through. Once he cleared the gate on the other side, he repeated the process, this time reattaching it. Emma gave him a curious look as he climbed in beside her.

"If we're coming back through here later," she asked, "why bother closing the gate?"

Colt shifted into first. "The field we just left—the cattle grazed it last week. Nothin' to it but nubs. It'll need a month or so to recover. Cattle don't care. They always think the grass is greener on the other side of the fence." He nudged Emma with one elbow. "We spend a lot of time rebuilding fences." He let the engine idle while he grabbed a hammer and nails from the back of the truck. A couple of taps tightened a loose strand of wire. Returning to the car, he spotted a small herd of deer.

"Look there, Bree," he said, aiming a thumb toward several does and their young parading across the road as if they didn't have a care in the world.

"Oooooh, I see one with spots." Bree bounced in her seat.

"That's a fawn. She was born this past winter, and she's just a baby." He pointed to a slightly larger doe whose spots had been replaced by tawny-brown hair. "That's her sister. She's a year older."

Bree settled against her seat back. "I want a sister. Mommy, can I have one?"

The hint of color that rose in Emma's cheeks sent his thoughts in the direction he'd been trying to keep them from going ever since the first day they'd met. He shook his head. Though he had to admit the image of Emma on the front porch waiting for him to come home at night was a tempting one, he wasn't ready to settle down. Or was he? He goosed the gas pedal so hard, Emma nearly ended up in his lap.

"Hang on." He laughed as if he'd planned the move. "We're gonna go for a while."

Dark green grass brushed the sides of the little car as they bumped over the narrow, rutted road.

"Why don't you let me drive us through?" Emma asked when he stopped to open the next gate.

Surprised, he turned to her. "You drive a stick? The clutch on this one's awful stiff."

"I told you my dad was military," she said without explaining further. "Trust me, I can handle it."

"I bet you can," he said, pitching his voice low and loving the way her tongue darted out to lick her lips. "C'mon, Bree. You wanna help?"

Bree scrambled out of her seat so quickly he had to jump to keep up with her. The little tyke watched, seemingly fascinated, as he unthreaded the chain. He wished he'd thought to bring a camera when she threw her weight into helping him swing the gate open. He could get used to the warm, fuzzy feeling he got whenever he showed the kid the basics of ranching, the way his dad had taught him, he thought, as Bree stuck to his side while Emma drove the Rhino through. It must have been the bright sun that made his eyes water, he decided. He swiped a hand over them as he climbed back into the ATV.

Emma canted her head and gave him a worried look. "You feeling all right?" she asked.

"Yeah. Must've swallowed a bug or something." He cleared his throat while he worked to get his feelings under control. What would it be like for Bree to grow up without a dad? No one to take her to the father-daughter dance. To eventually walk her down the aisle. His stay on the Circle P was a short one, he reminded himself. It wouldn't be fair—to Emma or Bree—if he got too close, too involved in their lives when he knew he'd be moving on.

For the next while, he mostly stuck to his job as tour guide, though he couldn't help tackling a few small problems along the way. When he pointed out the long rolls of silage they'd feed the cattle over the winter, he made quick work of taping a few holes in the blue plastic covering. At the cement watering trough, he paused again, this time just long enough to adjust the guide wire on the solar panel array.

"Ready to see the cattle?" he asked and smiled when Bree clapped her hands. In the north quarter section, most of the herd had spread out on the other side of a fence. He drove until he found a shaded spot before he stopped to let everyone stretch their legs.

"Who's up for a snack?" he asked, pulling a small cooler and an old quilt from the storage area.

"Are there cookies?" Bree asked expectantly.

Colt tugged on one of the little girl's pigtails. "Nah, I'm not a good cook like your mom." He sent Emma an approving look. The breakfast she'd rustled up that morning was more in line with the Circle P's traditions. "It's just cheese and crackers and sweet tea," he said. He unrolled the blanket under the tree. "You want some?"

"Uh-huh." Bree plopped down beside him while Emma helped him dole out the snacks. "Mr. Colt," Bree asked, "why do the cows have earrings?"

Colt looked up from the thermos to study the herd. The little girl was right. The bright orange tags hanging from each ear did sort of look like jewelry. He cracked a smile. "Cows don't have names. Their tags are how we keep track of them."

"They have to have names," Bree declared. "Look, Mrs. Wickles. That one's Spotty. There's Blackie. That's Red." After asking permission, she took her doll closer to the fence, where she continued assigning pet names to every cow in sight.

Colt slanted a look at Emma. "You know we raise *beef* cattle, right?" For her benefit, he added, "The tags contain microchips that hold detailed records for every head—parentage, birth weight, how much they've grown at certain milestones, vaccinations. If we need data on a single cow, we run a scanner over the tag and download the info straight onto the computer."

"That sounds like a lot of paperwork," she said, pointing out the obvious. "Who handles it?"

"My dad did it all." The cattle shimmered. A hard knot formed in his chest. "I'll never be the man he was," he said, his voice ragged, "but I'll do my best."

"I remember the first time I wanted to hang a picture after Jack died. It's tough, doing things that were always someone else's responsibility."

"Yeah." He let his gaze drop to a pair of dark eyes, where understanding glistened. Emma's fingers stroked his wrist. He cleared his throat. "Yeah, well, tracking the cattle, that's one of my jobs now. We used to jot everything down by hand. It's easier with the scanners. 'Course you still spend hours pulling your hair out over it."

Smile lines deepened slightly around Emma's mouth. She reached up and tugged on his hat brim. "Looks like you've got plenty."

Colt stretched out, munching on a cracker. "I imagine it'll be a might gray around the edges by the time Royce and Randy take over. The day-to-day operation is enough to keep us all busy, but we're already startin' to plan the winter cattle drive. Birding tours, too. The folks from *Beaks and Wings* said they might be interested in doing a feature article." Bird-watchers all over the world subscribed to the glossy magazine.

"It's beautiful here." Emma waved a hand. "Restful. You must love it."

He swept his gaze over the familiar scene and tried to see the place through her eyes. Like cotton balls, white clouds dotted a sky that was more turquoise than blue. Distant trees provided the only break in perfectly flat land that rolled to the horizon. Wind danced across the field of fresh tall grass. He heard the cattle pulling and eating, and suddenly it hit him: this was home, his home. In all his travels, there'd never been another sight or smell or sound exactly like it.

"I do now," he managed.

She paused, a small frown niggling her perfect lips. "Why did you leave?"

"Chalk it up to being young and foolish, I guess." Colt helped himself to another cracker. "Then Dad died and…and things changed. Suddenly, what I was doing didn't seem so important anymore."

"But you don't see yourself staying on permanently?"

Was that a wishful look in her eyes? Colt leaned back

on his elbows, his boots crossed at his ankles. There was a test hidden somewhere in her questions. He wasn't sure he could pass it, or that he wanted to, so he stuck to honest answers. "I've thought about getting my own place. Raising bulls for the rodeo. Maybe I will…one day."

"You're a natural for this kind of work, Colt."

"Because I'm big and strong?" Teasing, he flexed his arm.

Emma shook her head. "I had no idea there was so much work involved. Here you're giving me a tour of the ranch, but you haven't stopped working from the time we left the barn."

After making sure the cattle still captured Bree's attention, Colt leaned down to steal a kiss. "I wouldn't exactly call this work."

She placed her hands flat against his chest. "Hmm, nice. But I'm onto your ways. You're trying to distract me."

"Am I doing a good job?"

Cicadas buzzed, their low drone providing a pleasant background to the quiet sounds of cattle chomping on the thick grass. It felt right, slipping his arm around Emma's waist while Bree stood at the fence. Soon, a calf wandered over to investigate the visitor and, for the next few minutes, the two youngsters entertained each other. The opportunity was too good to pass up, and Colt stole another kiss. Okay, maybe it was three.

All the while, he told himself he should get moving. The thousand and one responsibilities he'd shouldered as manager of the Circle P waited for him back at the ranch house. He needed to check up on the workers, make sure they were doing the jobs he'd assigned them. Instead, he held Emma a little closer, enjoying the feel of his hand round her waist, her slim legs pressed against his own.

For the life of him, he couldn't think of anywhere he'd rather be.

Chapter Nine

They had to stop. Now, before things went too far and she lost her heart to the man with the tumbleweed existence. The one who shared too many traits in common with her late husband, her father. The one whose goals in life didn't include the house, the family, the roots that were so important to her.

Yes, there was more to Colt than she thought at first, and his kisses—oh, how they made her ache for more. But, summoning a strength she didn't know she possessed, Emma reluctantly pulled away.

"I think we'd better head back. I hear people expect dinner on the table at six each night." She traced the inside of his arm and silently begged him to deny it when she added, "They tell me the boss is a stickler for tradition."

Much to her chagrin, he offered no resistance. His mesmerizing eyes lost their dreamy quality. He pushed himself to his feet, rounded up the remains of their snacks and stuffed the trash into a garbage bag, which he slung into the back of the ATV.

Dusting off his hands, he turned to her. "If we leave now, we'll have time to swing by the little house. The boys say it'll be ready for you and Bree by tomorrow."

Emma stood, still holding the blanket where she and

Colt had recently traded kisses. Moving out of the main house meant no more wandering down the stairs on a sleepless night to wind up on the couch with Colt. Not having his scent waft out at her every time she opened the closet. An end to the dreams that came from her head on his pillow. While the promise of a place of her own had drawn her to the Circle P, the little house couldn't make up for all the advantages of staying right where she was.

But moving was the smart thing to do. The only thing to do, since letting herself get closer to Colt would only lead to heartbreak when he realized they had different goals for the future. Ignoring the little voice inside her heart that argued maybe she should have thought of that before she kissed the man, she summoned Bree from the fence where her daughter had spent the past fifteen minutes making friends with the calf.

"Hey, sweetie, let's go."

"I can't, Mommy. Baby Girl needs me to feed her." Bree held out a handful of freshly torn grass.

Any thought of arguing with her died when Colt swept Bree high into the air. "Baby Girl, huh? That *bull* calf has to learn how to eat all on his own. Next time we come back to check on him, you'll see. Soon, he'll be bigger than you are."

"Tomorrow? Can we come back tomorrow?"

Colt lowered the little girl to her feet and tickled her belly. "Maybe not tomorrow, Little Bit. I have work to do." When Bree's features clouded over, he sank to his knees. "Next, we're gonna see your new house. Tomorrow after supper, if it's okay with your mom, I'll take you for a ride on a horse."

Her daughter's body slammed into Emma's thighs. "Please, Mommy. Please, please, can I?"

Nodding, Emma turned away so neither of them would notice the sheen of tears in her eyes. The man might be bossy and arrogant, but Colt, with his kind heart and solid values, would make a wonderful influence in her daughter's life. But the man who could steal her heart just as easily as he'd stolen her breath was leaving. After the first of the year, he'd return to his rootless life with the rodeo. A life she wanted no part of.

Taking the coward's way out, she left Colt to cajole her daughter into the Rhino while she finished folding the blanket. Her thoughts were still a jumbled mess when she slipped onto the front seat. The vehicle dipped to the side as Colt slid behind the wheel. While he drove, she drank in the stark beauty of land that rolled to the horizon broken only by the occasional palmetto or pine tree. In less than a week, she'd fallen in love with the Circle P. And if she were honest with herself, she'd admit she'd fallen for the man on the seat beside her, too.

EMMA DIDN'T SAY much on the ride back, but Colt wasn't worried. From the horror stories his married friends told of house-hunting trips, he supposed she was two parts excited and one part anxious about her new home. Not that she had anything to worry about. The sturdy cottage had been his parents' before they moved into their spacious suite in the main living quarters. Built from concrete blocks, it had survived countless hurricanes with barely a scratch.

"It's not the Taj Mahal," he admitted, pulling onto the driveway that was little more than a flattened strip of crabgrass. A carport jutted out from the house like one of the horn buds on the calf Bree called her new, bestest friend. He stopped beneath the awning of corrugated fiberglass, where he let the engine idle just long enough to treat himself to a glance of Emma's shapely legs.

"Don't worry 'bout the yard. I'll have one of the guys throw down some seed." He lifted his gaze to study bare patches of gray sand. It'd take a ton of fertilizer before his cows would bother busting a fence to get at the so-called grass. "On second thought, we'll sod it. I bet Sarah will part with some of her orchids and other flowers when she gets back. Won't be long before the place is fixed up all pretty."

To his surprise, Emma waved a dismissive hand. "Don't bother. I doubt I'll spend enough time here to justify the effort."

His stomach knotted. "Leaving so soon?"

An odd look flitted across her face. After a pause that lasted a split second too long, she gave her head a shake that was only somewhat reassuring.

"Most mornings, I'll need to be in the kitchen by sunup," she explained. "It'll be dark before I get back. It doesn't make sense to waste time and materials on a yard when no one's going to be here to enjoy it."

He'd have sworn there was more to her story but she had a point. A quarter mile from the main building, the little bungalow really wasn't much more than a place to lay her head at night. When the thought of Emma in bed stirred an entirely different interest, he pictured them walking home hand in hand at the end of the day, then hanging out for a few hours before they disappeared down the hall to the bedroom. But something about the image didn't work, and he stopped himself. A long trek after an exhausting day in the Circle P's kitchen? Yeah, that was exactly what the doctor hadn't ordered. Especially when it meant slapping mosquitoes and dodging the local wildlife along the way.

Besides, there was Bree to consider.

Troubled, he swept his hat from his head and shoved a hand through his hair. Once school started, all the youngsters on the Circle P would catch the bus at the end of the road each day, but what about summers and holidays? He'd never spent much time around kids, but even he knew that leaving a four-year-old alone in the house wasn't a good idea. And wrenching Bree from her bed before dawn every morning didn't sound much better. Stuck with a plan he wouldn't have chosen, he stretched his legs as he got out of the Rhino.

"This house is yours for as long as you want. The boys have worked hard all week to get it ready." He thought it best not to mention the years' worth of spare equipment, tools and supplies they'd hauled out of the place.

Falling behind as they reached the uncovered patio not only let him slip his arm around Emma's waist, but gave her an unobstructed glimpse of the interior. With Bree trailing in their wake, they stepped into the freshly painted living room.

"Whew!" Even he had to admit the paint fumes and the heat were a bit much. He strode to the thermostat, where he moved the selector to a spot somewhere between frigid and bone-chill. Outside, the ancient air handler Garrett had tinkered with roared to life. From the vents in the ceiling came the faintest breath of over-heated air. A stink of mildew swirled into the room.

A curse formed on Colt's lips but he caught it before it spilled into little ears. He crossed to the windows and pried them open.

"It'll be better when the house airs out some," he apologized.

Emma swiped a light sheen from her forehead. "How hot does it get in the summer?" she asked with a half laugh. She brushed a few flecks of blown insulation from a rickety end table.

"I had the guys bring some stuff out of storage." He frowned at a lumpy couch that didn't look nearly as inviting as the leather sofa where he and Emma had traded kisses that morning. Down a short hall, he grimaced when Bree's bedroom door squeaked open.

The little girl peered tentatively from the doorway. "I like my room now better." She slipped her hand into Emma's.

Out of the mouths of babes. Colt scanned four bare walls that held all the appeal of a prison cell. His shoulders sagged.

Clearly trying to make the best of the situation, Emma broke in. "How 'bout if we paint the room a different color? Maybe pink? Or yellow?"

Bree's thumb found its way into her mouth.

His confidence flagging with every step, Colt showed Emma her room, noting the swallow she took before she pronounced it *great.* There wasn't enough elbow grease in the world to completely strip fifty years' worth of wax from the worn linoleum.

"Can we see the rest?" Blinking rapidly, she backed out of the room.

The Formica-topped table in the breakfast nook had to be forty years old if it was a day. Though Emma did her best to conceal it, he caught her quick, dismayed gasp when she spotted dials on an electric stove manufactured long before the digital age. Frost clung to the icebox in an ancient refrigerator. Suddenly parched, he started to get himself a drink of water. Rust stains in the sink convinced him to come up with a better idea.

He squared his shoulders, his decision made. No matter what his parents' intentions, or what Ty and Sarah had in mind, they'd put him in charge of the Circle P. As such, he had a say in who lived where. And this—he took in the kitchen that needed far more than a lick and a promise—wasn't fit for Emma and Bree.

"You know what?" He swung Bree up in his arms. "Now that my brothers have gone, there are plenty of spare rooms in the main house. You two should stay there. When Ty and Sarah come back, I'll talk to them about making different arrangements."

Relief spread over Emma's face. It disappeared almost before Colt registered it.

"We can't put you out like that, Colt. For better or worse, this is what I agreed to when I accepted the contract your dad sent me."

"You deserve better," he growled. Balancing Bree on his hip, he pulled Emma close. "Let me make sure you get it. Till then, you can stay right where you are." A half dozen small houses dotted the Circle P property. He'd pick the best one and give it a major overhaul.

"In your room?" Emma struggled out of his grasp. "That's not right, either."

He shrugged. "It's only temporary. I can move into Mom and Dad's suite, or even—" he gestured "—here."

When he thought about it, moving to the little house wasn't such a bad idea. Being around Emma stirred an itch he wouldn't be able to deny for very long. Unless he was seriously mistaken, she felt the same way, too. Which meant, sooner or later, they'd wind up in bed together. But that was something he figured she didn't want any more than he did. Least ways, not until they knew where they were headed.

No, he shook his head, it'd be better for all of them if he was the one to move.

Refusing to argue the point, he shepherded them back through the living room and out the door. Once they were safely away from the house, he whipped out his phone. "Josh, let's get that air-conditioning guy out here this afternoon. Have him install a whole new unit in the little house."

He could deal with the rickety furniture, the rust-stained water, the bare white walls. But if he was going to move in, he needed ice-cold air. Thinking about Emma—in his bed or not—already had him in a sweat. He couldn't deal with that and the heat, too.

"ARE YOU SURE this is what you want?" Emma gave in to a last-minute shiver of doubt. "You don't have to."

Bree gazed up at her as if her mom had suddenly sprouted an extra head. "I been wanting to do it my *whole* life."

"All four years of it, huh?" Kids. Who knew they could be so dramatic. Or patient, for that matter. While Emma had prepared dinner this afternoon, Bree had only asked how long it would take Colt to finish his chores a dozen times. Or was that two? She'd lost count somewhere around one o'clock. After that, moving Bree into a room of her own had helped. Her daughter had spent at least an hour arranging her dolls *just so* on a shelf in what used to be Randy's room. Still, it had taken all her parental tricks and then some to keep the child occupied until Colt finally knocked on the kitchen door at sunset.

"Yes, Mommy." The brim of Bree's miniature Stetson bobbed up and down in time with her solemn nod. "I'm gonna be a *real* cowboy."

"Cowgirl," Emma corrected. She grinned at the shiny red boots Colt had unearthed from a trunk in the attic. "Sounds like you're ready, then."

As Colt led Star from the barn, the four-year-old scrambled to the top rail. Emma slipped an arm around her daughter's waist to keep the little girl from bolting into the corral. Beneath her hand, Bree's body practically throbbed. Not that Emma could blame her. She felt a little anxious herself. Well over six feet tall and solidly built, Colt had always impressed her with his strength and size. Yet, Star's long head rose above his. Four large hooves, perfect for kicking little girls, plodded through the sand. The idea of letting her baby get anywhere near the big animal suddenly didn't seem like the smartest move. Torn, she swung back to Bree.

Canceling the child's first horseback ride would break her daughter's heart. But what if her little girl fell? What if she kicked and screamed and started a stampede?

A stampede? It was only one horse. Now who was being dramatic?

Emma swallowed past the lump in her throat. *Take a breath,* she told herself. To steady her nerves, she focused on the rancher who'd sworn he'd keep her daughter safe. Colt had earned a powerful physique through years of hard work and bull busting. More important, the man didn't make idle promises. If he said he'd keep Bree from harm, he would. Pure and simple.

She watched her daughter slip a tiny hand into the rancher's larger one. So much trust glowed in the little girl's dark eyes that it made Emma feel all soft and warm inside. She gulped. If she didn't watch out, she'd lose herself to the man she'd once practically accused of being an arrogant bully. Safeguarding her heart would be so much easier if she'd been right about that first impression. But Colt had another side. A tender side. A side that had won her over, despite frequent reminders that *love* and *forever* weren't cards in the hand they'd been dealt.

She'd spent a lifetime waiting for a man like Colt. His kisses made her feel alive. His touch played with her senses. His low voice toyed with her emotions so much she'd even considered sleeping with the man just to get it over with. But she sensed that making love to Colt would be like eating a single potato chip. Though people swore they could stop after just one, no one had the willpower to walk away.

She was pretty sure she didn't.

So, no. There'd be no sleeping—or not sleeping— with Colt. Not now. Not ever.

It was the best way, the only way, to keep from falling in love with the man.

Yeah, you just keep telling yourself that.

"Look at me, Mommy! I'm riding!" With Colt's strong arms wrapped around her, Bree waved from her perch astride Star.

Thankful for dark sunglasses that hid her watering eyes, Emma summoned a smile. She waved and quickly pointed the camera. She'd had those two arms around her own waist. She knew the strength in them. Better still, she knew how much Colt cared for her daughter.

"Do you see me, Mommy? Are you watching?"

Emma lassoed her wandering thoughts. Her fears that Bree might overreact and cause a problem were proven groundless by the little girl who hung on Colt's every word. The child who often displayed the attention span of a gnat grew even more focused with every trek around the corral. That didn't stop Emma from holding her breath when Colt turned the reins over to the child, but Bree handled them as if she'd been guiding a horse all her life.

The sun's last rays reflected off golden clouds by the time Colt lifted Bree from the saddle. He doffed the little girl's hat and sent the beaming child toward the gate. Seconds later, Bree rushed into Emma's outstretched arms.

"This is the best day of my life!" her little drama queen gasped. "Did you see me? Can I see the pictures? Can I? Can I?"

"I'm so proud of you." Emma aimed a kiss for Bree's cheek and missed, landing it on the little girl's nose. "We'll play the video on the TV before you go to bed tonight."

From the far side of the corral, Colt inclined his head. "Daylight's wasting," he called.

Pressed into babysitting service, Josh pushed away from the rail where he'd been watching with Chris and Tim. He moseyed over and leaned down to Bree.

"You know, there's an owl in the barn. She's made her nest up in the rafters. If we're real quiet, we might get to hear the baby owls chirping."

Bree stared up at him. "We had pigeons where I used to live. I got to feed them," she said importantly.

"Columbidae." Josh nodded. "We don't have a lot of those here, but we have other kinds of birds. Flamingos and spoonbills and ibis and…"

"You know a lot about birds, Josh?" Emma interrupted before Bree lost interest.

The young man's ears pinked. "Yeah. It's kind of a passion. Mr. Ty, he likes 'em, too. I showed him the best nesting areas. We're gonna camp out there for the Audubon Society's bird count next winter."

So the boy was a budding ornithologist. She wondered if Colt knew.

"Can we see Maize's puppies, too?" Bree tugged on her new friend's hand.

"Sure," Josh agreed. "Now that their eyes are open, you can hold one of them. If you're real gentle."

"I will be," Bree promised.

Under the careful watch of the two kitchen assistants and Josh, Bree skipped toward the barn while Emma stepped into the corral. Sand shifted over the tops of her sneakers and, within seconds, she understood why everyone on the ranch wore boots. But any thought of shopping for a pair faded when she peered up into Colt's face in the fading light.

It wasn't just the thought of taking her first horseback ride that had her heart tripping over itself. A desire to trail her fingers along the stubble that graced his firm jaw stirred within her. She wrenched her gaze away from deep-set eyes to study the perfect lips that were mouthing instructions.

The horse. Yeah. She was here to ride a horse. It took some doing but she whipped her attention to the matter at hand.

Grasping a handful of mane the way Colt showed her, she hoped she didn't look nearly as awkward as she felt when she stuck one foot into the stirrup. Colt's hands at her waist boosted her confidence enough that she gritted her teeth and bounced into the air. And then, just like that, she was up. Her leg cleared the horse's wide rump.

Leather creaked and the saddle shifted ever so slightly as she swung her way into it. She stabbed her free foot into the other stirrup before she looked down.

"Whoo!" she gasped as the realization that she was so high atop a living, breathing animal sent a wave of vertigo crashing over her. She clutched the pummel with two hands. "I don't know about this…" she began.

Before she could finish, Colt swung onto the blanket behind the saddle. His torso pressed against her back, sending an electrifying current straight through her. She heard the sharp intake of his breath, felt the slight tightening of his forearms and knew he felt the same thing.

Colt cleared his throat. Rather than leaning down to kiss her as she hoped he would, he clucked gently at the horse. Star moved at once. The animal's rolling gate startled a laugh out of her chest. Soon, though, she was mesmerized by the horse's gentle sway, the jangle of metal, the plodding sound Star's hooves made despite the loose sand.

"I could get used to this," she breathed.

"Our horses are well trained." Colt's matter-of-fact answer whispered through her hair. "That doesn't mean they won't try to get away with something every once in a while, so you need to know what you're doing when you're around them."

Though her hands felt like they were all thumbs, he gave her the reins. "Horses' mouths are sensitive. A gentle tug is all that's necessary to tell them the way you want to go."

She was sure she'd fail. Sure the big horse wouldn't listen to a single word she said, much less a tug on the reins. But Colt believed she could do this, and once again, she reminded herself how much she trusted the big rancher. With his fingers at her waist he talked her through a series of figure eights. To her growing amazement, Star responded to her every command.

"Now pull up on the reins," Colt said long after the last glimmers of light had faded from the sky.

She did as she was told, and Star plodded to a halt.

"You done good." Colt's arms wrapped her closer to him. "Next time, you can ride him all by yourself."

"Oh, I don't know about that," Emma hedged.

Colt tsked. "Sweetheart, everybody on the Circle P rides. It's part of what we do."

"Yeah, but..." She took a breath. "I like this." She snugged his arms tighter around her waist. "I kind of wish things would stay the same."

Even as she said the words, she knew they could never come true. Colt wasn't here to stay. His life was on the road, his future tied to the PBR, his stint as manager of the Circle P a short one. Trouble was, the more she pictured the permanent home she and her daughter would make on the ranch, the more certain she was she'd wind up with an unhealthy helping of broken heart to go along with it.

Because, despite her best efforts to the contrary, she'd fallen for Colt Judd. And she'd fallen hard.

Chapter Ten

"They're putting Arlene in the hospital till the baby comes." Once firm and strong, Doris's voice trembled.

"But that's months away. Isn't Arelene's due date sometime in October?" Air whistled between Colt's teeth. He bent beneath the weighty news. Garrett had to be going out of his mind, he thought. His mother, too. He pressed the receiver closer to his ear. "You need me to come? I can be there tomorrow."

"No, son. You stay and take care of the ranch. Knowing it's in your hands, that's a huge load off my mind. Especially with Ty and Sarah gone. Have you heard from them?"

"Not a word." But then again, he hadn't expected to. The owners had made it pretty clear nothing less than a hurricane or wildfire were reason enough to interrupt their much-delayed honeymoon. So far, Colt hadn't placed a single call to the fire department. With any luck, Ty and Sarah would return before the storm season began.

"And our new cook? Is she working out the way your dad thought she would?"

"Emma?" Colt asked as if he needed a reminder. "She's fine."

Better than fine, actually. Ever since that first sleepless night, he'd made a habit of wandering into the kitchen once Bree was tucked in for the evening. While Emma concocted something reasonably close to one of the Circle P's famed dishes, he relished his role as her official taste tester. So far, he wouldn't call their experiments a rousing success, but that was okay. They weren't in any hurry. Besides, he didn't mind helping out. Not as long as he could steal the occasional kiss. Or find an excuse to brush against Emma's slim hips. Maybe trace a lazy circle across her shoulders. Afterward, they invariably ended up on the couch, where the woman's kisses left him hungry and aching for more.

Despite a growing urge to take things to the next level, he'd resisted. And why was that, he wondered. He'd certainly knocked boots with one or two gals back when he was rodeoing, though he'd left those days behind when he hung up his bull rope and gold buckles. Being around Emma stirred a sense that he could have it all, as long as white picket fences and wide front porches were part of the package. Something that, lately, he'd considered more and more.

Suddenly aware that long seconds had passed while his mom waited for him to continue, he cleared his throat. There were some topics even a grown man didn't discuss with his mother. His relationship with Emma was one of them. He let the subject of the new cook drop.

"Give Arlene and Garrett my best. Tell 'em I'm prayin' for 'em."

Before he had a chance to follow through, the phone rang again. Colt straightened out of a weary slouch as the representative from *Beaks and Wings* apologized for calling so late. He squinted at a clock that told him several hours stretched before suppertime. He was still trying to figure out what the guy meant when, without further warning, he found himself knee-deep in a discussion about arrival dates and shooting schedules. A glance at the calendar nearly made his knees weak— would have, if he'd been standing—but he kept his doubts to himself. Instead, he asked a few questions and jotted even fewer answers while he offered assurances that, of course, the Circle P could host a weekend trail ride in—he gulped—four days. Hanging up five minutes later, he drummed his fingers on the desktop.

Did the unexpected visit from a major birding magazine qualify as *flames* or *storms?*

He told himself it did not and set to work. He'd just finished jotting down a long list of tasks when the dinner bell sounded. He sniffed the air, noticing for the first time the tantalizing aroma of his favorite dish. Grabbing his notepad, he strode toward the kitchen. Over the past three weeks he'd softened his approach with the men, but this—he shook the pad of paper—this changed things.

His gaze landed on the pork chops Emma had prepared. Thick and browned, they were probably fine for anyone else's table, but they definitely weren't Southernfried the Circle P way. He took in the rest of the buffet and kicked himself. He'd been so wrapped up in his growing fondness for the new cook he hadn't paid enough attention to the important stuff. The impending arrival of special guests meant everything on the Circle P had to be perfect, including the food. Which, from what he was seeing, looked too much like it came from a froufrou New York restaurant and not at all like the ranch's traditional hearty fare.

Biding his time, he pushed food around on his plate while the ranch hands ate their fill.

"Listen up," he said, coming to his feet before everyone scattered in different directions. "I've got good news, and I've got bad news." He didn't wait to ask which they wanted first, but plunged ahead.

"You all know how hard it is to keep a spread the size of the Circle P afloat. Opening up our spring and winter roundups to tourists, that's given our bottom line a considerable boost. Ty—Mr. Parker—wants to add to that by taking folks on bird-watching tours. He's already started advertising them. Which is why I'm talking to you now. I just got off the phone with *Beaks and Wings*."

At the mention of the magazine most folks considered birding's version of the *National Geographic,* Josh's head rose. Colt scanned the long table. No one else seemed to care.

"Seems they've run into a problem with their summer issue. They need to reshoot it, and…they've decided to give us a try. So we're going to hafta pull together a trail ride for them." He paused for a beat. "The reporter and photographer will be here Friday and Saturday."

"What's the good news?" one of the men shot back.

At his place near the end of the table, Josh's brow furrowed. "I thought *was* the good news."

The boy's comment drew hoots of laughter from the older hands.

"The good news," Colt corrected, "is that ya'll draw time and a half for the weekend. The bad news is, startin' at first light tomorrow, we're gonna be busier than a pickup rider at the rodeo."

He let the grumbling die down before he started handing out assignments. "Josh, you get down to Little Lake. The trails have grown over since the spring cattle drive.

Trim the bushes back far enough that we can ride two abreast."

To his surprise, Josh shook his head. "Mr. Colt, this ain't the right time of year to trim those bushes. The birds eat the berries."

The kid had the audacity to argue with him?

Colt squelched a comeback and moved to the next item on his list. "Tim and Chris, we're gonna want a big campfire Friday evening. Make it happen. The house-keeping staff'll scrub the bunkhouse by the lake from top to bottom." He went on, finally reaching the last—and most difficult—item. He toughened his stance.

"Emma, there's a menu for the trail rides posted on a clipboard in the pantry. Make sure you stick with it." He gestured toward the tiny peaks the cook had piped around a nearly empty bowl of mashed potatoes. "None of this fancy stuff. Just good, plain food and plenty of it. That's what the Circle P's known for."

From the way Emma flinched, he'd have thought someone slapped her. Maybe he'd been a touch too harsh, he admitted, but a good review from *Beaks and Wings,* or better yet, landing on the magazine's list of premier birding destinations, meant money in the Circle P's coffers. He wouldn't let anyone, not even the woman who'd stolen his heart, stand in the way.

HER MOUTH DRY, Emma stared at Colt. To say these past few weeks had been the best of her life, well, that was an understatement. Having Bree at her side during the day and listening to her daughter's sweet now-I-lay-me-down-to-sleep at night were simple pleasures she'd longed for during their hectic years in New York. As for her work, seeing the Circle P's hungry ranch hands scarf down every morsel she put in front of them ignited a warm spot in her chest.

Best of all, though, were the nights Colt joined her at the stove. They'd spend hours cooking, tasting, adjusting—and, yes, kissing—while they struggled to re-create a favorite dish. Afterward, they'd tiptoe into the great room. There, they poured a glass of wine, a beer, some sweet iced tea. They talked—about their lives, their dreams, their hopes for the future. And they kissed. Oh, how they kissed. The man could take her breath away with a single hooded glance.

But, from the instant she'd spotted the pages of the cookbook in their watery bath, she'd known this day would come. She'd done everything possible to delay the inevitable. She'd slaved over the ruined recipes, carefully peeled the pages apart, smoothed and, even, ironed a few. She'd used a magnifying glass, consulted restoration experts, searched the Circle P from top to bottom in hopes of finding a scribbled copy, a note, anything that would help her make sense of faded and smeared ink. Through it all, she'd prayed that when it finally came down to a choice, Colt would choose her over the traditions of the Circle P.

But this list. At least one of the recipes on it was lost forever.

She fanned her face with the slip of paper. Okay, so she'd made mistakes. She'd faced a learning curve when she first came to the ranch. Men who performed hard, physical labor ate more than the diners in upscale restaurants. She got that. She adjusted.

Still, she knew food. Just as important, she knew how to impress a food critic. Hadn't tour guides and reviewers visited Chez Larue practically every night of the week? She knew without a doubt that the people from *Beaks and Wings* wouldn't be satisfied with Colt's plain-food-and-plenty-of-it mantra. Any more than they'd be happy trekking through miles of palmetto and pine trees without spotting the spoonbills Josh had mentioned.

Pondering this last, she plunged her hands into her pockets and waited until the shuffle of boots across the floor faded. When the screened door slapped shut behind the last ranch hand and they were alone, she turned to Colt.

"Can we talk?" She barely got the words out before his hand chopped the air.

"The menu's set, Emma." The face she loved hardened into stubborn lines that weren't quite as lovable.

"Not that. Can we talk about Josh?" Waiting, she folded her hands below her waist. If Colt would change his mind about this, maybe, just maybe, he'd consider the compromise she really wanted him to make.

His eyebrows slanted together. "What's he got to do with anything?"

She deliberately kept her voice soft and low. No matter how much she just wanted to help, she was venturing into an area that technically wasn't any of her business. "Did you ever think Josh might be right about not trimming the bushes?"

Colt only shook his head. "I've told you before, the kid's lazy."

"It could be that," she conceded. "Or…" She took a deep breath and let it out slowly. "You've been concerned that he doesn't fit in here at the Circle P. But he knows more about birds than anyone else on the ranch. More than Ty, even. I think he could help a lot while the people from *Beaks and Wings* are here."

"You sure about that?" Colt's eyes homed in on her.

She noted the way he spun his hat in his hand, a movement he made whenever he was uncertain. At last, he scuffed his foot against the tile floor.

"The kid's always got his nose in a book. Come to think of it, they're all about birds." He glanced up, his blue eyes considering. "I'll talk to him. What else?"

"I know you want this menu." She tapped one finger on the list. "It's tradition, and I understand that. I wouldn't dream of changing it. But this recipe for Brunswick stew? I don't have it. It's not in the cookbook. It must have been one of the ones we lost."

Thunderclouds darkened Colt's blue eyes. He sank heavily onto a chair. "What are we going to do?"

"Your mom probably knows it by heart. Is there any chance we can ask her?" She had no idea how they'd get the recipe out of Doris without revealing how badly the cookbook had been damaged, but it was a risk she was willing to take. For Colt's sake, and for her own.

Her heart slid into her throat when a world of worry seemed to settle across his shoulders. Without meeting her eyes, he shook his head. "I don't see that happening. Arlene's in the hospital till the baby comes."

"Oh, Colt." That changed things. "I'm so sorry," she whispered, thankful she'd breezed through her own pregnancy. "Well, there's nothing for it, then. I'll just have to do the best I can. I'll work on it and have something for you to taste test tomorrow afternoon. I'll have some other things I want you to try, too." The instant his posture stiffened she signaled him to stop by holding up her hands. "For now, don't decide anything. If you like the new dishes tomorrow, we'll serve them on the trail ride *in addition* to the traditional fare. If not, well…"

The alternative was too painful to think about, the words too horrible to say out loud. She didn't want to destroy the Circle P's customs; she wanted to expand them. To do that, she needed Colt's blessing. But his tight hold on tradition left no room for negotiation. What kind of future could she have with a man who never compromised?

COLT EASED OPEN the screened door and slipped into the kitchen. The wooden frame firmly in his grasp, he guided the door closed. He held his breath as the lock snicked into place before he spared a glance at the woman on the other side of the room. Emma's shoulders remained loose. Her hips swaying slightly, she stirred something that smelled just this side of divine on the stove.

Certain he'd escaped her notice, Colt allowed himself a few seconds to enjoy a view that was better than the sun coming up over the pasture. Emma had captured her hair in a ponytail. The ends brushed lightly against her shoulders in time to music only she heard. The heavy white coat she'd worn the day they met hung from a hook near the pantry. She'd traded it for a figure-hugging T-shirt over shorts that exposed enough smooth white skin to make his mouth go dry. He imagined untying her apron, discarding it in a crumpled pile on the floor while she slipped into his arms. They'd kiss, feast on each other until they both were completely sated.

Across the kitchen, a spoon clattered to the stove top. The noise jolted his thoughts back to the present as Emma turned to face him.

"Ready for a taste test, cowboy? Or are you just going to stand there all afternoon?"

A saucy smile told him she'd caught him staring. Colt gave an unashamed grin in return. Eager to bring Emma into sharper focus, he crossed the room to where she stood. He checked to see if they were being watched.

"Bree around?" he asked when he didn't spot the little girl.

"Playing with dolls in her room."

Emma's careless shrug didn't fool either of them. The teasing light in her eyes practically shouted that she was as eager for what came next as he was. The tiniest fleck of tomato dotted her cheek. Telling himself he'd be remiss in his duties if he didn't remove it, he stepped forward, his thumb already brushing her chin. As long as he was this close, he thought stealing a kiss would be in order.

One kiss turned into a half dozen. They were both panting lightly and in danger of getting in over their heads right there in the kitchen by the time he summoned a hard-to-find resolve. He crushed Emma to his chest and rested his chin atop her head.

"Oh, woman, what you do to me," he murmured into her hair.

"Me?" She snuggled closer. "And here I thought you were the one with the magic touch."

For a few minutes, he relished the feel of her slender form in his arms, the softness of her curves, the rapid beat of her pulse. Eventually, though, his heart rate slowed enough that he started thinking clearly again.

"I guess we'd better get to it," he suggested, hoping she'd insist on staying right where she was. Disappointment lanced through him when she broke their embrace. Emma straightened her apron, a bemused look on her face, her hair slightly mussed.

"Ready to try the stew?" She tucked an errant curl behind one ear.

He nodded, when all he really wanted was to sweep her off her feet and carry her up the stairs. But they weren't randy teenagers, not caring about the when and the where, and only concerned about the what. There'd be no slipping away to his borrowed room down the hall. Any more than he'd sneak into hers and run the risk of Bree wandering in on them in the middle of the night. No, when they made love the first time, he'd surround Emma with satin and white lace, plush pillows on a soft mattress, champagne and caviar.

He glanced at the calendar over her shoulder and groaned. The days until Ty and Sarah's return stretched like an eternity. He wasn't sure he could last, but he was determined to try. Emma was worth waiting for. The first chance he got, though, he'd whisk her away to someplace special for their first, but certainly not their last, official date.

In the meantime, there were recipes to refine and guests to impress and a ranch to run. Still, he couldn't help being pleased at the way her hand shook the tiniest bit when she ladled the stew into bowls. He grinned, knowing their desires were in sync.

Taking a helping, he blew on his and tasted.

"It's good. Really good," he pronounced, rolling the meaty sauce around on his tongue. He probed the bowl, noting corn and the Circle P's signature snap beans. "I thought you didn't have the recipe."

"I don't." Emma's shoulders straightened ever so slightly. "From what Chris and Tim told me, I figured out the basics. The rest is all tinkering. Is it thick enough?"

"That part's fine." Colt tried another spoonful. "There's something missing, though."

He gave the matter considerable thought while he looked over the ingredients spread across the counter. In his role as guinea pig, he'd learned how minced onions gave a dish more flavor than chopped ones. To appreciate the subtle difference between Tabasco and hot sauce. He fought the urge to slap his forehead. That's what this dish needed to make it perfect—more hot sauce. He picked up the bottle.

Doubt filled the look Emma gave him as he added a few dashes to the pot and stirred.

"Perfect!" he declared after taking another taste. The smell made him ravenous. He checked his stomach. As suspected, his hunger had nothing to do with food and everything to do with the cook.

Spatula in hand, she said, "Now, about that dessert…"

"Banana pudding?" He leaned in to kiss the tip of her nose.

"You don't think it's too plain? It's such a simple dish," she said, as if that was a bad thing.

"It's tradition." He shrugged. "The first night out, it's always stew and corn bread. With banana pudding for dessert."

Emma drummed her fingers on the countertop. "Listen, I want you to try something. But to do it, you have to close your eyes. No peeking."

"That doesn't sound like any fun." He sent a lingering gaze up and down the length of her.

Emma crossed her arms, her voice stern. "I mean it."

Dutifully, he did as he was told. He might have cheated just a little when he heard her open the refrigerator door. But he wasn't interested in what she pulled from the shelves. No, he was more interested in watching Emma. She was grace personified and he knew that if he spent the rest of his days watching her, he'd be well and truly a happy man. The realization that he'd fallen in love with her struck him and he blinked, knowing he couldn't imagine a future without her and Bree in it. He squeezed his eyes tight the instant she turned toward him.

"Okay. Now, open wide," she ordered after a clatter.

"Wait a sec." He clamped a hand over his mouth. "Give me a clue here. Salty or sweet?"

"Sweet," she said at last.

He grinned then. "Nothing could be as sweet as you."

"Oh, you." Her breath washed over him in a long sigh that stirred desires of a different sort entirely. "Hush now, and take a bite."

Cold. Wet. Sweet. The sensations landed in his mouth. He chewed, taking his time the way she'd taught him while the flavors separated into familiar tastes. Graham crackers. Bananas. Vanilla.

"I don't need to guess," he declared. "Banana pudding."

"Good. Now, hold on a sec. I want you to try something else."

He licked his lips, hoping that what came next was a kiss. Emma's were so sweet he was pretty sure he could survive on them and them alone.

Sugary sweetness exploded on his taste buds. Banana, yes. Vanilla, yes. Something dense and chewy had replaced the Graham crackers. He caught a hint of caramel, a nutty crunch. Whatever she'd laid on him wasn't a kiss, but it was definitely the next best thing. His eyes popped open and took in Emma's smiling face.

"What was that?" He stole a quick glance at the containers she'd pulled from the refrigerator. Of course, he recognized his mom's banana pudding. Simple. Wholesome. Beside it sat a pie of the sort he'd never seen before. He stroked a finger along the edge and licked. "Mmm." Whipped cream from a can couldn't hold a candle to Emma's homemade.

"Banoffee pie," Emma pronounced. "My take on it anyway. I want to serve both on the trail ride this weekend."

Colt crossed his arms. He glanced from one dish to the other. A feeling much like disloyalty stirred within him. He fought it down. Really, he asked himself, what was the harm in serving both?

Chapter Eleven

The sun beat down from a cloudless blue sky. Despite the light breeze that rippled through the saw grass like waves, sweat seeped from beneath Colt's cowboy hat. It dribbled down his neck as he studied the sea of green, searching for the anhinga Josh had pointed out to Dave. The photographer's camera clicked furiously. Meanwhile the journalist, Mike, jotted notes astride Daisy. It wasn't until Josh led the way onward, toward what he promised was an impressive site, that Colt managed to spot the dark gray snakebird sitting on the ground, its wings partially unfolded. The stance reminded him of the way Emma often propped her hands on her hips… and his focus swerved away from birds and trail rides to the one thing guaranteed to raise his temperature.

Emma. When had he fallen in love with the woman? The day she stood toe-to-toe with him after Bree's run-in with Three? The moment he spotted her bravely facing down alligators in order to protect her daughter? Or was it later yet, when she let her guard down long enough to let him glimpse the vulnerable woman underneath? No matter. He loved her and, the first chance he had to be alone with her, he intended to tell her how much.

"You coming, Mr. Colt?"

He looked up to see that Josh and the two men from

Beaks and Wings had moved on without him. His mus-
ings over, he tipped his hat to the waiting bird, clucked to
Star. With a jangle of tack, the big horse trotted through
the brush to catch up with the others, who were nearing a stand of tall, skinny trees. There, saw grass gave
way to patches of palmetto so dense the fronds rustled
against Colt's stirrups as he followed the others into
the welcome shade. Once they stepped beneath the first
trees, however, the undergrowth thinned. Pine needles
carpeted the ground. They muffled the horses' hooves,
but from somewhere up ahead came a noisy squabble
of what sounded for all the world like crying babies.

Star's head came up. His upper lip curled. In quick
succession, the horse blew air and snorted. Seconds later,
Colt caught a whiff of something foul.

"We'll go on foot from here." Josh reined to a halt
near the center of the grove. Among the dark green
pines, he pointed to one coated in bird droppings. "How
close do you need to get?" he asked Dave.

"I'll probably have to climb up for the best shot."

"Whew! You're gonna get a might ripe," the boy
warned. "Remind me to stay upwind of you on the way
back."

"All part of the sacrifices we make for art." Leather
creaked as the photographer dismounted. He dug in his
knapsack, coming up with a second camera. "You want
to snap a few?" he asked Josh.

"Sure." Apparently forgetting the smell, the kid
turned to his boss. "Unless you'd like to do it, Mr. Colt."

Colt gave the air a surreptitious sniff. Why anyone
wanted to climb the slick white limbs in order to peer
into a nest while very large, very angry birds tried their
best to change his mind was beyond him. But Josh's

earnest expression told him the boy was dying to do just that.

"Josh is our resident ornithologist. I wouldn't be near as much help," Colt admitted. Settling in to wait, he had to give the kid credit. May wasn't the best time for birding. Even he knew that was in winter, when huge migratory flocks flew down from the north. The season hadn't stopped Josh. He'd led the team from *Beaks and Wings* to dozens of nests, including at least three that belonged to endangered species like the wood stork.

"Join us, Mike?"

"Up there?" The journalist glanced away from his notes with a wry grin. "I'll help Colt take care of the horses. It'll give us a chance to talk about the Circle P." He twisted in his saddle. "You don't mind, do you?"

"Sounds good." Before they'd left the ranch house, he and Josh had worked out a system. The boy would answer questions about birds and their habitats, leaving him to deal with everything else. He swung his gaze away from the two enthusiasts who trekked toward the tree. "What can I tell you?"

"I've studied your website and brochures. No need to cover that ground again." Mike flipped through pages in his notebook. "Any problems our readers should know about?"

"We're not trying to hide any secrets. The trip you're taking is just a short version of the same experience we give all our other guests." Colt shifted, trying to find a comfortable position on a saddle that grew prickly under the journalist's intense stare. "Fire away. What do you want to know?"

"I understand the ranch's long-time manager passed

away recently," Mike said, diving straight into the interview. "How's that going to affect things?"

"My dad." Colt's chest tightened as a thousand memories came rushing back. So much for expecting the man to lob a few softball questions. Mike had gone straight for the jugular. "He taught me and my four brothers everything there is to know about ranching and raising cattle. The Judds have a long history on the Circle P. As do the Parkers. Our families aim to keep on doing things the way they've been done for four generations."

"That's good to know." Mike scribbled a few notes. "There've been other changes. I hear your cook turned the kitchen over to someone new."

"Emma. Emma Shane." Colt bit back the smile that came to his lips whenever her name was mentioned. He gulped as jumbled bits of his life fell into place like pieces in a jigsaw puzzle. Emma had stolen his heart, made it hers forever. She made him want to settle down, to trade the traditions of the Circle P for ones they'd start on their own ranch.

Could he make it happen?

Between his winnings from the rodeo and his savings, he had enough set aside to buy some land. Someplace close by in case Emma wanted to continue on as the head cook at the Circle P. He wouldn't give up the rodeo. Not entirely. But instead of always being on the road, he'd raise bucking bulls. Horses, too. He'd become a livestock supplier. Eventually, he'd supply rodeos throughout the South.

"You were saying?"

Colt blinked. "Emma. Yeah. She's been with us for about a month now and—"

"Is she available?"

"You want to ask her out?" Colt met the reporter's gaze head-on. "She's a widow," he said slowly, "with a four-year-old daughter." He passed the reins from one hand to the other. Not many men would be interested in a ready-made family. He sure hadn't been. Now, though, he couldn't imagine a future without Emma and Bree in it.

He smiled, thinking how Bree's eyes would light up when she got her first pony. Or later, when she graduated to her first horse. If the child took after her mom, she was going to break a lot of hearts when she got a little older. Signing on as her dad would probably mean more nights than he could count pretending to clean his shotgun in the living room when some would-be Romeo showed up on the front porch. Was he up to the challenge? A new certainty in his chest said *Yes*. He and Emma would help the girl—their daughter—find her way, and they'd do it together.

He paused when thoughts of Bree's future happiness opened a door to other things the child wanted. Like a baby brother or a baby sister. Maybe a slew of them. The fun Emma and he would have trying to make that happen. His gut tightened and he resettled his belt to lessen the pressure of an ache he'd grown familiar with ever since Emma stepped into his life.

"I didn't see any children."

"Bree's with a babysitter back at the ranch," Colt practically growled. He eyed the journalist. The guy was in for a rude awakening. Emma was spoken for.

Except she wasn't. And with a gulp, he told himself he'd better get right on that.

Beneath him, Star shifted nervously. Colt ran a soothing hand down the horse's neck.

"Relax, man." A wide smile broke across the journalist's face. "I don't stand a chance. I saw how it was with you and her the minute you introduced her. You're a lucky man."

"I aim to be." The world lost its greenish tint as he reached a decision. Before the night was over, he'd square things between him and Emma. There were words that needed to be spoken, promises to give. Only, what if she didn't feel the same way?

He cast a look over his shoulder. The camp where countless Parkers and Judds had slept during every spring roundup was a little over a mile away. Having traveled in ATVs specially designed to look like covered wagons, Emma and her staff would be there already. Soon, she'd turn the supplies they'd brought down from the main house into a meal fit for their special guests.

A meal that would have to wait a little, he told himself the moment he spotted Josh and the photographer traipsing toward them. Both men wore a generous layer of guano. He might not know much about birds, Colt acknowledged, but he knew the lay of the land. A short ride would take them to fresh water that bubbled up from an underground spring. Tapping Star's sides, he led the way.

He smiled, knowing the circuitous route they'd follow back to the bunkhouse would give Emma and her helpers extra time to prepare for their arrival. After a long day in the saddle, Colt could think of little else besides a shower and a good meal. That and seeing Emma again. He crossed his fingers, trusting that the preparations for dinner had gone smoothly.

Once the horses were groomed and bedded down for the night, he headed for the bunkhouse, where kerosene lanterns glowed from windowsills. Accustomed to eating off paper plates at the rough-hewn tables, he blinked in surprise at the red-checked tablecloths and sturdy dinnerware Emma had hauled down from the main house. More surprises waited on the buffet. Though he spotted the stew and corn bread served on every trail ride, there were additions he didn't expect.

Hunger pangs shot straight through him when he noted a platter of pork chops—crispy and golden and just the way he liked them. He restrained an urge to dig in, focusing instead on the fancy edging along a bowl of mashed potatoes, the tomato roses in the salad. An enormous rib roast sat on a carving board surrounded by grilled vegetables.

What happened to good, plain food and plenty of it? He held his breath as he searched the desserts at the far end of the table. Air seeped slowly between his teeth when he spied the bowl of banana pudding flanked by three kinds of pies.

"It looks like our cook got a little carried away with dinner tonight," he offered, eyeing a small mountain of butter balls for the corn bread.

"Wow!" Dave quit rubbing his hands together and reached for the camera that was never far away. "If you put on a spread like this every night, you won't have any trouble getting return business."

Mike grabbed a plate. "Where'd you find this new cook? I swear that looks like burgundy sauce." He spooned some over his corn bread and sniffed. "Mmm," he said, closing his eyes. "Smells like it, too. Will you ask the chef to join us?"

Colt glanced longingly at the pork chops. "Sure thing." He abandoned his own plate on the serving line while the crew of ranch hands they'd brought along on the trail ride filed in. Stepping around the divider and into the kitchen, he called to Emma. "Can you come out here for a minute?"

A frown wrinkled her brow. She wiped her hands on a dish towel. "Problems?"

"Just the opposite," Colt said, overcoming his own misgivings. "I think you have some new fans."

Her chef's whites hung on a nearby peg. She shrugged into the jacket he hadn't seen her wear since she first arrived on the Circle P. The moment she slipped her arms into the sleeves, her demeanor changed. Gone was the laughter he loved seeing in her eyes. A cool professionalism took its place, making her look for all the world like the few chefs he'd seen on TV. Buffeted by second thoughts, he gulped. Would she want to spend the rest of her life on a ranch? With him?

He watched her walk slowly to the end of the serving line, where she greeted each of their guests by name before folding her hands at her waist. "What questions can I answer for you?"

Mike sopped up the last of his burgundy sauce. He pulled a spiral pad and a pen from his pocket. "Where did you train, for one thing."

"Two years at the Culinary Institute in New York," she said, naming a school so famous even Colt had heard of it. "Followed by two more working my way up to sous chef at Chez Larue."

"Those are impressive credentials." Mike looked up from the notes he'd been taking. "Not to dabble in clichés or anything, but what's a great chef like you doing in a place like this?" The man gestured to the walls of the log cabin. "Shouldn't you be in Miami or Atlanta?"

As anxious to hear the answer as the journalist, Colt

dropped a hand over his own stomach lest its growling announced his hunger to anyone within hearing distance.

"While working in the top kitchen in New York was a challenge and a thrill, it didn't leave much time for family life," Emma answered without missing a beat. "The Circle P offered peace, quiet and a chance to run my own kitchen."

"Well, you certainly got what you asked for." Mike stabbed his pen toward the window. A day's ride had taken them far from any sign of civilization.

"Yes, well, we do have internet and phone service at the main house." A modest smile stole onto her lips. "Out here, not so much."

The answer drew a chuckle from the photographer, who'd finished snapping pictures and hunkered over his meal as though someone might steal it from him. "You gotta taste this beef, Mike. It's like butta, it's so tender." Clearly savoring every morsel, he cast star-filled eyes at Emma. "Chef, your talents are wasted out here in the middle of nowhere. You move to the city, I guarantee every table in the house'll be filled every night."

Mike clicked his pen and slid it into his pocket. "And entertainment?" he asked, taking a plate. "What does a gal like yourself do for fun?"

On that note, Colt moved in to disrupt the conversation before their visitors had a chance to entice Emma back to the big city. "You should eat before your food gets cold." He let his gaze tighten enough to put the man on notice to back off. "The boys'll have the campfire going if ya'll want to mosey on outside after."

Turning to Emma, he asked, "You want to bring the fixin's for s'mores out in a little bit?" He wasn't about to leave her alone with these guys. Not for a minute.

Though she gave him a curious look, Emma followed his cue. Claiming she had a kitchen to clean and breakfast preparations to get underway, she left them to their meal. After a dinner that exceeded all its hype, the idea that Emma might one day wish to return to her life in the city weighed heavily on Colt as he joined the men from *Beaks and Wings,* Josh and several other wranglers at the fire.

"You like what you do?" Colt chose a seat beside Mike. Thanking heaven for a brisk breeze that kept the mosquitoes at bay, he stretched his legs toward the flames.

"Love it." Mike grabbed a stick and poked the fire. "Next week, we're headed to Canada. After that, who knows? There's always a challenge. Like the time we…"

While the reporter launched into a story, Colt drummed his fingers on the log. Not too long ago, he'd always been on the go, too. But his ideas for the future had changed as his feelings for Emma had deepened. Now he could think of nothing better than settling down with her. Together they'd make a home for Bree. He looked up just as Mike finished regaling Josh with a story about the trials and tribulations of wildlife photography.

"Easy for you to say." Bravado glowed from Dave's face. "I didn't see you skinning a tree over a gorge in order to get the shot of that bald eagle."

"Good thing Florida doesn't have cliffs." Josh laughed and slapped his leg. "What we do have—we have roseate spoonbills and more ibis than you can shake a stick at. If we head out before sunrise in the morning, I promise you'll get your cover picture for your magazine."

Wanderlust filled the kid's eyes. Colt wondered how

long before the boy struck out, aiming to make his own way in the world.

"Before daybreak, you say? That'd be, what, four-thirty? Five o'clock?" At Josh's nod, their two guests stood. "Guess we'll turn in," said Mike.

"You won't stay for the s'mores?" Colt rose to his feet.

Dave patted his stomach. "After all that good food tonight, I won't be hungry for a week." He turned to face Colt. "She ever opens her own place, you let me know, man. I'll make a standing reservation at her restaurant."

"It's a shame she's stuck out here where no one will realize how talented she is," Mike added with a sorrowful look. "You know, she could practically name her own price at any restaurant in Miami or Atlanta. They'd climb all over themselves to get her in their kitchens."

"She'll appreciate hearing you think so highly of her," Colt responded, though the remarks sent a tremor of self-doubt down his spine. The guys made it sound as if, no matter how much Emma loved the Circle P—or him— she'd eventually regret not making a name for herself somewhere else. But that wasn't true, was it? Another shiver ran through him at the realization that, one way or another, he'd find out soon enough.

"Long day." Emma stretched, working the kinks out of her back after a day filled with the kind of nervous tension she hadn't experienced since leaving New York. Very aware of the brooding male presence beside her, the one who hadn't taken her into his arms the moment she joined him at the fire, she spread her fingers to absorb warmth from the flames.

"What did you think about dinner?" She hated having to drag it out of him, but she couldn't wait another minute.

"It was good." Colt's shoulders rose and fell in a shrug that was anything but careless.

"But…"

"But I thought you were going to lay off all the frills and stuff."

She folded her arms across her chest. She'd worked extra hard to provide a memorable meal. And, from the comments Mike had made, she'd hit her mark. "Asking me to serve plain food, that's kind of like asking a bull rider not to wave his hat."

The analogy got Colt's attention just as she'd known it would. "I scored that meal a ninety-three."

According to what she'd learned about bull riding, a ninety-three would take home the prize purse. "High praise from a man who once protested every change." Colt had softened his stance on tradition, developed a willingness to try new things. Not that he was the only one. She had a deeper appreciation for the customs that turned a house into a home, a piece of property into a heritage to be passed from one generation to another. She grinned up at him when he turned toward her. His blue eyes probed her own.

"You been studying up on rodeo, have you?" A smile played at the corners of his lips.

"I might have caught a few episodes on ESPN," she admitted. "Some of those cowboys are h-o-t." She fanned herself.

A large helping of green-eyed envy mixed with the humor in Colt's eyes. "Never thought of you as a buckle bunny."

"A what?" She laughed and prodded a muscular biceps.

"You don't even want to know." Colt cleared his throat. "Mike and Dave suggested your talents were wasted on the Circle P. That you could do better somewhere else."

"I've had offers," she admitted. After ruining the Circle P's cookbook, she'd circulated her résumé. A four-star in Fort Lauderdale had offered full control of their kitchen, plus a nice salary bump. "But I like it here." She gestured toward the darkness beyond the fire. When Colt slung one arm across her shoulders, she peered up at him, batting her lashes like a doe-eyed schoolgirl. "If I'd known you back then, would I have been jealous?"

"Nah." Colt rested his chin atop her head while they watched the fire. "Some of the guys, they knocked boots with every filly that gave them a come-hither look. Me, I never saw the appeal in all that casual sex. There were women—I'm not a saint. But I reckon I hadn't found the right one." He paused then, his arm slipping around her waist while his long fingers possessed her from hip to breast, exactly the way she wanted. So softly, she almost missed it, he whispered, "I have now, though."

"You trying to say something, cowboy?" She snuggled closer.

"Yeah, I guess I am. I love you, Emma Shane. I want us to be together."

Tears stung her eyes. She blinked them back. She'd known from the moment Colt stepped in front of her, shielding his mom from the truth about the ruined cookbook, that underneath his gruff exterior, he hid a soft, tender heart. One she could love. Her feelings had deepened with every second they'd spent together over the past month, every kindness he'd shown Bree. At some point—she couldn't pinpoint when exactly—she'd realized she'd fallen head over heels for this man, though she'd been reluctant to say the words until she knew for certain he felt the same way. Free to finally confess her own feelings, she exhaled slowly. "I love you, too, Colt Judd. More than I ever thought possible."

She squared around, her focus locked on the flames reflected in his eyes as he slowly bent toward her. The kisses he feathered across her forehead were entirely unsatisfactory. She longed to have his lips on hers, and tipped her face to his. Still, he hovered over her, teasing her with his breath, his closeness. Just when she thought she couldn't possibly wait another second, he leaned in for a kiss.

He tasted of vanilla with a touch of caramel that brought another round of tears to her eyes. Their tongues danced, and she twined her hands around his neck. She brushed her fingers through his hair, smiling as she recalled his insistence that the silky strands were in need of a trim. She inhaled. A feeling that she'd finally arrived slipped over her as she drank in a blend of sun and grass and Colt's own scent.

When he eased beneath the hem of her shirt, she gasped at the feel of his work-roughened hands against her bare skin. Each hard ridge, each callus, stirred sensations she'd never known before as he trailed his fingers over her waist. One by one, he climbed her ribs while her breasts tightened in anticipation. It had been so long— too long—since she'd felt a man's touch, and she gave herself over to the pleasure of each caress, reveling at being in the arms of the one she loved.

Soon, though, even that wasn't enough. Not by far.

The urge to touch, to feel his skin pressed against hers, grew so insistent she ran her fingers over Colt's thin T-shirt. Her heart pounding, she traced a seam to his belt and tugged. Her breath grew shallow, and she moaned his name when she finally pressed her hand against the hard planes of his wide chest.

She froze, gasping, when the screened door of the bunkhouse squeaked open. With a raspy thud, a log collapsed into the fire. It sent up a shower of sparks. Not fifty feet from where they sat, the door slapped shut. Boots scuffed across the dry grass as she and Colt stifled giggles while they hurried to straighten their clothes.

"Mr. Colt. Ms. Emma." Josh stepped out of the shadows, his bedroll in his arms. "Thought I'd stay out here tonight. Keep an eye on the fire. I probably won't sleep anyway. I'm too worked up about tomorrow. Ms. Emma, we havin' breakfast tomorrow? That dinner tonight was mighty fine, but I got a powerful hankering for your biscuits."

Emma used the time while Josh rambled to steady her breath.

"What time, Josh?" she said, smiling at a secret joke. She'd set Doris's blue tins aside lately in order to perfect her own biscuit-making technique. The ones she produced were lighter and fluffier. Better yet, the ranch hands craved them.

"Early." Colt cleared his throat. "Josh says we need to hit the trail before first light in order to see the spoonbills when they take off."

"I bet that's something." She tried to imagine thousands of birds taking to the air at one time, and failed.

"You should come with us, Ms. Emma. You won't

regret it, I swear." Josh unfurled his bedroll a short distance from the fire.

She checked with Colt, who nodded his approval. "Okay, then, I think I will." She eyed the young man whose presence had brought an abrupt end to Colt's kisses. "I'll need to get to bed, though, if I'm going to have things ready in the morning."

Colt stood, pulling her to her feet along with him. "Guess we'll leave you to it, Josh." His arm around her waist, he took a couple of steps toward the bunkhouse before he turned back to the boy. "Good job today."

The kid shrugged. "I had a great time. Mike and Dave, they seemed like they liked it, too."

"You know, if these birding tours are a hit, guiding them might turn into a permanent job for you."

"No more herding cattle?" The kid looked up, his eyes alight.

"Well, now. I wouldn't go quite that far." A deep chuckle bubbled out of Colt's chest. "We are a cattle ranch, after all."

"I reckon I could live with that." Josh plopped down on the bedroll, one arm crooked behind his head. "Night, Mr. Colt."

"Good night, Josh."

Emma leaned into Colt. "That was a nice thing you just did," she whispered once they were beyond earshot.

"From my dad's notes, I know he worried about the boy. Ty, too. He's young and hasn't exactly fit in on the Circle P. It's good to know we have a place for him." At the door, he paused before his eyes met hers. "You, too. I hope you'll make this your home."

"I'd like that," Emma breathed, amazed at how things had changed since the day she and Bree had driven onto the ranch to find themselves in the middle of a funeral. Not that long ago, she'd been sure she wouldn't last any longer on the Circle P than ice in a glass of sweet tea. As for finding the love of her life, well, Colt hadn't even been on her radar. But who knew that beneath all his bluster and endless moving around lived a man who wanted the same things she did—love, family and roots?

She leaned her back against the door. In a move that made her heart do a happy little dance, Colt propped one arm over her head. He bent to plunder her lips, drawing back far sooner than she wanted him to.

"If I asked to come inside…" he breathed.

"I'd say *what are you waiting for*," she murmured.

Gold flecks heated the look he gave her. "You don't know how much I want that, but not here. Not now." The look he swung down the hall took in the rooms on either side of hers, rooms occupied by their guests. "Sarah and Ty are due home next week. What say we get away for a while once they're back. I know of a real nice B&B in Saint Augustine. We could spend the weekend—" he traced one finger along her cheek "—get to know one another a lot better."

"A weekend?" Though his touch sent little shivers of pleasure racing down her spine, her heart thudded. Going away with Colt sounded like something this side of heaven, but she wanted more than a casual fling. She had to know if he did, too. "What exactly did you have in mind?"

"Girl, I love you. More than the air I breathe. You mean more to me than all the gold buckles I earned on the rodeo. I want you in my life. You and Bree."

If it was commitment she was looking for, he'd delivered it. They kissed then, a kiss filled with promises that they'd fulfill another day. But later, as she tossed and turned on the narrow bunk, Emma wondered if she'd made the right choice. Oh, she and Colt loved each other. No doubt about that. But the owners of the Circle P might not be nearly so forgiving about the ruined cookbook or the other changes she'd brought to the ranch. She worried a fingernail, concerned that she might be out of a job the minute Ty and Sarah arrived back home.

And then what? Could she and Colt make their relationship work if she had to leave?

The answer still eluded her when the alarm beeped. Downstairs in the serviceable bunkhouse kitchen, she pushed aside her worries to focus on the job at hand. She was up to her elbows in biscuit dough when Colt tiptoed into the room carrying his boots. He paused only long enough for a kiss, but that was enough. It settled her nerves and swept away the vestiges of doubt. While she slid trays into the oven, he headed out the door to help Josh saddle the horses. Boots thundered on the stairs by the time she plucked hot-from-the-oven biscuits off trays and slid them into insulated cases. She poured coffee into to-go cups while giving instructions on the rest of the breakfast preparations to a sleepy-eyed Tim.

Outside, the horses stomped their hooves. Their lips fluttered as they blew air like impatient old ladies while the riders mounted up. Confident in her new skills on horseback, thanks to the lessons Colt had given her, Emma swung into the saddle with an easy grace. The first streaks of pale light brightened the horizon as they set off.

The clear, cool air swept the cobwebs from Emma's head better than the strongest cup of coffee. Riding alongside Colt made it easy to chalk her restless night up to useless worry. Just as the sun climbed over the horizon, Josh reined his horse to a stop on a narrow beach at the edge of a lake that stretched as far as she could see. While Dave scrambled to the ground, camera in hand, Emma cast a wary eye along the shore, looking for alligators.

"Relax," Colt's voice whispered out of the darkness. "The horses'll let us know if we have anything to worry about."

She didn't have a moment more to think about it. From the dark water came the sounds of a thousand heavy smokers clearing their throats. The sun rose higher. The moment its rays glinted off the lake's surface, thousands of birds stretched their wings. A whooshing sound filled the air as they took flight, their huge pink wings turning the sky a vibrant coral. Feathers drifted in their wake. One floated in front of Emma. She snagged it and put it in her pocket for Bree.

Josh waited until the last bird winged its way out of sight before he cleared his throat. "This is just a hint of what we have every winter. Imagine that," he told no one in particular.

"It worked for me. You've outdone yourself, Josh." Mike's hushed tones drifted over the empty water. "You get the shot, Dave?"

"You betcha! That was awesome. Worth getting up for."

Emma tried to picture the astounding sight magnified tenfold and failed. She glanced around at the saw grass and palmetto revealed by the rising sun. Suddenly, she knew she'd found a home amid all the stark beauty. More than anything, she wanted to spend the rest of her life here. Raise her daughter here. Grow old with Colt here. Sure there were challenges. Things to learn and dangers to avoid. But she could trust Colt to keep her and her child safe. Just as, for the first time in her life, she felt certain she'd found the one person she could trust with her heart.

Chapter Twelve

A frown tugged at one corner of Colt's mouth as he pulled a battered suitcase from beneath the bed. Empty stock pens and a last-minute scramble to fill them for last week's rodeo in Tulsa had prompted a flurry of emails from the PBR. Their latest promised everything from first-class accommodations to a retirement plan if he'd come back to his old job. While he couldn't deny the ego boost, he shook his head. He was staying put. Buying his own place. Setting up house. With Emma, if she'd have him. In the meantime, though, the Parkers' return meant he'd run out of excuses for staying on at the main house. He stacked clothes from the dresser into the suitcase until a soft whine snagged his attention.

"This is Chocolate." Bree stood in the doorway struggling to hold on to one of Maize's puppies.

"Did you name him that?" Colt swept a hand over the top shelf of the closet, making sure he hadn't missed anything.

"Uh-huh. 'Cause he's brown. Like chocolate." The puppy clambered to lick her face. "Whatcha doing?"

He grabbed a handful of hangers. "I'm packing. I have to leave this afternoon."

"Are you going away?" Bree set the puppy on the floor. The dog scrambled for a pair of boots Colt had discarded at the end of the bed. Growling, the pup sprang for one.

"Hey, there, Chocolate. Them's my boots. They're not for eating." He checked the heels—clean enough—and propped the worn footwear at the end of the mattress. "Don't you pee on the floor now."

"Are you going *away?*" Bree repeated.

The panicky note in the girl's voice snagged his attention. "Mr. Ty and Ms. Sarah and Jimmy will be back home today. That makes a lot of people in one house. It's time for me to move out." He hoped Bree accepted the explanation. The real reason—that he couldn't sleep down the hall from her mom another night without taking things to the next level—yeah, that wasn't fit for four-year-old ears.

"My daddy went away." Bree squatted down beside the puppy.

Colt's favorite pair of Wranglers fell from his fingers. Fighting an urge to slap some sense into his head, he knelt beside the child. "Your daddy went to heaven. My dad's there, too." His throat thickened and he swallowed. "I'm not going that far. Just down the road a little ways." The puppy wandered in circles near the dresser. "Do you remember the other house? The one with a bedroom just for you?"

Bree gave a solemn nod. "Mommy said we'd paint it. I like pink. What's your favorite color?"

Colt eyed the child, who wore pink bows in her hair. "If you like pink, then that's my favorite, too."

"Good— Oooh! No, Chocolate!" Bree snatched the puppy off the floor, but the damage was done. A puddle spread across the wood. "I'm sorry, Mr. Colt. Don't be mad. That's a bad Chocolate. Bad puppy." She hugged the squirming ball of fur to her chest, her eyes tearing up.

"Hey, there." Colt petted the dog's nose. "He didn't mean anything by it, did you, boy?" For a moment, he let the little dog lick his fingers. "We'll clean the floor before the wood gets ruined."

Rising, he crossed to the bathroom, where he grabbed a handful of tissue. He studied Bree and her dog. "It takes a lot of responsibility to raise a puppy. You'll have to train him right so he'll be a good dog when he grows up."

Are you talking to yourself there, Colt?

As he mopped and blotted, he considered what the next twenty years might be like if he and Emma made things permanent. He'd have more than puppies to worry about, for darn sure. He pictured walking Bree to the bus stop on her first day of school. Practicing her lines for the Christmas pageant. He saw himself sitting in the audience, mouthing the words right along with her. There were bound to be scrapes and bumps and probably more than one broken heart before she learned to drive a car. Before he knew it, he and Emma would be nodding off in their easy chairs, pretending they weren't sleepy while they watched the clock the night of her first prom. One day, God willing, a nice boy would come along. He'd catch their daughter's heart the same way Emma had caught his. Through it all there'd be laughter and tears and...

He brushed his eyes against one sleeve. Raising a child up right took a lot more effort than raising a puppy. Was he ready for that kind of commitment?

"Did the pee make your eyes water, Mr. Colt? Mommy says it stinks, but it doesn't. Onions make her eyes water."

Colt took a deep breath and slowly exhaled. "The stink comes later. If you don't clean up right away. Tell you what," he said, disposing of the soiled tissues. "I'll walk you downstairs so you can take Chocolate outside to see if he has more business to do. I have to work in the office for a while, but then I'm going to get Mr. Ty and Ms. Sarah. When I come back, I'll bring a surprise."

He added a stop at the pet store for chew toys to his tasks for the afternoon. Kids and puppies went together like heat and humidity. As long as he was in the business of raising both, it'd be best if the dog learned to leave his boots alone.

A short time later, he logged the last of the receipts into the Circle P's financial sheet and hit the enter key. Done, he exhaled. The monthly reports on the cattle, all logged. Bills, paid. Paychecks, issued. Accounts, balanced to the penny. He mopped his face and checked the in-box before shutting down the computer. His heart rate kicked up at the *Beaks and Wings* logo on an incoming email. A feeling that was half apprehension, half elation swirled through him when he clicked the mouse and an advance copy of the magazine's review appeared on the screen.

He took a breath. Whatever the outcome, he was stuck with it. And so was the ranch because, according to Mike's note, the summer issue had already gone to print. The mouse made a soft click. Colt scrolled down. *Five feathers.* He leaned closer. The magazine's highest rating didn't change. He scanned the flattering article, but earning *Beaks and Wings'* designation as one of the top birding spots in America didn't hold his attention the way he thought it would. Instead, a sidebar drew his focus to pictures of exquisitely prepared food and a glowing report sure to put "up-and-coming Chef Emma" on the map.

Colt exhaled the breath he hadn't realized he'd been holding. Clearly, a celebration was in order. He stood, picturing Emma's face when he gave her the good news. Her eyes would darken. Her lips would widen in the smile she wore especially for him. He'd hold her close, and together, they'd dance around the kitchen.

Or...

His heart thudded. On the trail ride, he'd brushed aside the compliments Mike paid their cook, but this... Doubt unfurled in his chest as Colt stared at a photo of Emma in her chef's whites. Even before the *Beaks and Wings* article, one of the premier restaurants in Fort Lauderdale had offered her complete control of their kitchen. According to this write-up—he thumped the printout— Emma had the skills to make a name for herself as one of America's top chefs. A position she'd never achieve by hiding her talents away on the Circle P.

He ran a hand through his hair. He'd spent his time at the top. Enjoyed the years of fame and fortune that came with being the best bull rider in the country. Emma wanted fame, too. Hadn't she dreamed of having her own TV show? Her own restaurant? He shook his head. She'd never make that leap as long as she stayed on the ranch. Wouldn't strike out on her own as long as he held her back.

A sick feeling formed in the pit of his stomach as he realized what he had to do. Before his courage ran out, he faxed a response to his boss at the PBR and placed a call to his brother Hank. Then, summoning every vestige of strength he possessed, he called Emma to the office.

"What's up?" she asked from the doorway a few minutes later.

Knowing one glimpse of the trust and love in her eyes would rob him of his nerve, he dug deep for the bravery he'd needed back in the days when he made his living by riding bulls. "Come on in, Emma. Close the door."

The saucy smile she reserved only for him faded just a smidge as she edged her way into the room.

"Have a seat." He gestured to the chair opposite the desk while he leaned against the wall. "Where do you stand with dinner preparations for the Parkers?"

At his formal tone, Emma's brow furrowed. Looking very much like the professional chef she was, she folded her hands the way he'd seen her do countless times. "I thought we'd serve rib roast, from the Circle P's own beef, of course. It makes such a beautiful presentation. Chris and Tim are prepping vegetables for the grill. There's a raspberry torte I've been wanting to try for dessert. Why? Was their flight delayed? We can push everything back if we need to."

Colt ground his teeth until they ached. The elaborate meal was as far from "simple food and plenty of it" as it could get. Though he knew every morsel would melt in his mouth, the menu made his task easier in a way. Maintaining his distance, he managed to say the hard words. "I know this is going to come as a shock, but I have to let you go."

"Go?" Confusion swam in the dark eyes he longed to see when he woke every morning. "Go where?"

His determination wobbled, but he forced himself to stay strong. "The meal you've planned for tonight only goes to prove what I've said all along—you'll never fit in here. The people at *Beaks and Wings* recognized it right away. See for yourself." He sent the pages he'd printed spinning across the desk.

Cowboy up, he told himself when his knees threatened to buckle.

EMMA DIDN'T EVEN glance at the papers Colt slid toward her. Briefly, she squeezed her eyes shut. Hiding behind the mask of indifference she'd honed through years of listening to her father's, her husband's, other chefs' rants, she buried the hurt that threatened to crawl over her face.

Hoping to get through to the man she'd fallen in love with, she asked, "What's this all about, Colt?"

When he refused to meet her gaze, panic beat its wings in her chest. Then, and only then, she reached for the magazine article Colt had tossed her way. Despite their raves during the trail ride, had Mike and Dave dissed her cooking? She worried her lower lip.

"They gave us five feathers!" she protested.

"They gave the Circle P five feathers," Colt corrected. "They hailed you as the next Julia Child. And they're right. You certainly don't belong on a ranch in the middle of nowhere, Florida."

Was that pain in his eyes?

A tiny spark of hope flared in her chest. Maybe Colt thought, somehow, he was firing her for her own good. If so, she'd prove him wrong. "I'm not going anywhere, Colt. I love it here. This is our home, mine and Bree's. Yours, too. I thought..." Her words faltered. Hating the needy note that had crept into her voice, she took a breath. "I thought we were going to build our future here. Together."

"You were wrong about that." Colt bit off each word as if he were tearing into a tough piece of meat. "The

PBR has made me an offer I can't refuse. I leave to-morrow."

Leaving? Going back to his life on the road?

Emma blinked, her hopes and dreams wavering. Time and again, Colt had proven that underneath his rough exterior beat the heart of a man who doted on her, on her daughter. He hadn't put it into words, not precisely, but she'd assumed they were making plans. Plans for the future. Their future as a couple, as a family. They'd talked about the ranch he wanted to buy. The bulls he intended to raise.

She swallowed, straining to remember what, exactly, he'd said, but all she could recall were the words he hadn't spoken. Words like *forever* and *always*. Nausea rolled through her midsection. She clamped a hand over her mouth.

For a second, she thought Colt's shoulders had slumped. She blinked, and realized she'd been mistaken. A cool reserve radiated from his rigid jawline. Instead of softening, his stance only firmed. The arms that had once held her close were now folded across his chest, shutting her out.

"It's time we face the facts and get on with our lives. My future isn't on the Circle P. Yours isn't, either."

Emma reeled back against her chair. If she didn't know better, she'd think the man she'd spent the past month falling in love with had never existed. In his place stood a stranger. One who looked remarkably like the angry man who'd yelled at her—twice—the day she'd arrived at the Circle P. In a callous voice, he said the words she'd dreaded then, but hadn't seen coming today.

"You're fired. Pack your bags and get out. I want

you gone by the time I get back from the airport with the Parkers."

White noise roared in her head. Her thoughts sluggish, she stared at Colt. At first, she'd been certain this was all some kind of joke, but his tone cut through her fog like a hot knife through butter. Hearing the harshness in his voice, she knew. Knew he'd fallen out of love with her as quickly as they'd fallen in love with each other.

A hollow spot yawned in her chest where her love for Colt was supposed to be. Rising on legs that felt far older than their twenty-six years, she carefully picked her way out of the office. In the great room, she trailed her fingers over the back of the couch where she and Colt had traded the most amazing kisses. She spared a single glance for the staircase he'd carried Bree up the nights her daughter had fallen asleep in his arms. Her head down, Emma trudged through the long hall lined with pictures of Judds and Parkers, the hall where she had hoped to one day hang a photo of her and Colt and Bree.

She glanced at the cedar walls of the house that had become her home and knew Colt was right about one thing. He'd done her a favor by firing her. She couldn't stay here. Not on the ranch where she'd found love and happiness. Without Colt, the Circle P was a wonderful place, a place where she wanted to raise her daughter. But it took the rancher to make it a home.

Summoning a calm she didn't feel, she drew her cell phone out of her pocket and dialed the number for a restaurant in Fort Lauderdale. She winced at the thought of stepping back into a bustling kitchen where tempers flared as often as burners under the pans. She nearly sobbed when she considered uprooting her daughter again.

But, honestly, did she have a choice? Her hands shaking, she informed the voice on the other end of the line that his new chef was on her way.

Finally, she drew in a courage-laced breath, squared her shoulders and pushed her way into the Circle P's kitchen a final time. In one corner Chris chopped veggies with the precision of someone who'd been born to the job, while at the pastry counter, Tim decorated a cake for the Parkers' homecoming. A cake someone else would have to serve because she and Bree were on their way out of here. A wave of homesickness for the ranch she was about to leave threatened to knock her down.

"Chris, Tim, I'm feeling a little under the weather," she announced from the doorway. "I'd appreciate it if you could carry on with the dinner preparations."

"You okay, Ms. Emma?" A worried frown crossed Tim's face.

Buying time, she closed her eyes and nodded. "I'm leaving the kitchen in your capable hands."

For a few seconds, she concentrated on staying upright, on ignoring the searing pain that gripped her heart. She spared a quick look at the small corner table where her daughter was coloring a welcome home banner for the Parkers. Her chest tightened and she swallowed her tears. For Bree's sake, she wouldn't cry. Wouldn't let her heartbreak show.

"I'm making a present. See?" The sign Bree held up had more scribbles outside the lines than inside them.

Emma lifted a hand, intending to brush it through hair she'd snagged into a bun in deference to the rising temperatures. She settled for tucking one of the pins in deep enough that it scraped across her scalp.

Yipping, a puppy scratched at the screened door.

"Chocolate!" Bree looked up from her artwork. "You're s'posed to be with your mommy and your brothers in the barn." Golden-brown from the days she'd spent playing outside, her daughter rushed to the door. She scooped the dog of indeterminate breed into her arms and carried him inside. "Mommy, look, he runned to me. Watch. I'll show you his new trick." Eight pounds of squiggling fur poured out of her arms when she bent over. "Sit, Chocolate," Bree ordered.

The dog plopped its heavy hindquarters on the floor.

"Now, shake."

The appropriately named puppy slapped one paw against Bree's outstretched hand. With a squeal of delight, her daughter scooped the dog back into her arms. "Mr. Colt said a dog is a big job. But I teached him good, didn't I, Mommy?" She patted the dog's head. "I'm gonna teach you lots of tricks, Chocolate."

Another wave of pain knifed through Emma's chest. When she and Bree left the Circle P, they'd have to leave the pup behind. Taking over as head chef meant impossibly long days that started late and ran far into the night. No, she shook her head. There was no way to fit even a small pet into their new schedule. And, from the size of his paws, Chocolate was going to be anything but small. She dropped to her knees and let Bree think she was letting the dog lick her face when, in fact, he washed the tears from her cheeks.

JUST WHEN HE thought Jimmy couldn't bounce any higher and still remain strapped in, Colt turned off the main road onto the long drive to the ranch house. "Keep your boots on," he told the youngster whose presence had stifled the serious talk he needed to have with Ty and Sarah. "We'll be there in a minute."

Beside him on the passenger's seat, the Circle P's owner stretched his long legs. "I can't wait to sleep in my own bed. Hawaii was nice, but nothing beats coming home."

Home.

Theirs, but not his. Not for much longer. The pain of leaving, of letting down all the people who were counting on him, was a knife in his chest. Colt stared through the windshield at land that had been worked by four generations of Judds. Thanks to Emma, he'd rediscovered a love for ranching that had been handed down from father to son. A love he wanted to pass along to children of his own someday. He wanted…this, he admitted as he studied barbed wire and green grass. Trouble was, having his own patch of saw grass and palmetto didn't hold the same appeal without Emma at his side. Before he could have what he wanted, he'd have to get over losing her. Have to reach the point where he could think about her without doubling over. Which, by his reckoning, might not happen till he hung up his spurs for the last time.

"Well, I want a decent cup of coffee." Sarah gave one of the ranch hands a friendly wave. "I missed the gurgle of our old percolator in the mornings."

"About that…" Colt swallowed past the lump in his throat. "Emma called it a monstrosity. She tossed it. The new one, though, it makes a mighty fine cuppa joe."

"You don't say."

Sarah leaned back so far into her seat Colt barely caught a glimpse of her raised eyebrows in the rearview mirror. Maybe he should have argued longer or stronger for the battered coffeemaker. He'd intended to. One look at the excitement in Emma's eyes when she lifted the new one out of the box, though, and all his objections had simply melted. The same way they had when she rearranged the cupboards. Or offered the men a choice between apples and oranges in their lunch pails.

"I know I promised to uphold the Circle P's traditions, but that old pot—"

"Nothing stays the same forever," Ty interrupted. "Look how much the ranch has changed. Five years ago, we raised beef—prime Andalusian cattle—and nothing else."

"And you were barely keeping body and soul together," Sarah pointed out.

"Lettin' tourists come along for the spring and winter roundups put us in the black and kept us there," Ty finished.

"Don't forget my flowers," Sarah chimed in. "With that end of the business doing so well, we can afford to take on two more foster kids this fall."

"Sounds like the birding tours'll be a big hit, too, thanks to Josh. He did a great job showing Mike and Dave around." Colt aimed for a parking spot among the usual assortment of pickup trucks and four-wheelers. "You'll have to read the article from *Beaks and Wings*."

"First thing on my list after we unload." Ty unbuckled his seat belt with an audible sigh.

"I can't wait to see Maize's puppies. Can I go to the barn, Dad?" Jimmy popped his door open when the truck rolled to a halt.

"Let the dog get a whiff of your scent before you go bustin' in on her," Ty cautioned the same way Colt had taught Bree. "Remember, you've been away for a while."

The boy who'd acquired a deeper tan in the month

he'd been gone slowed his steps just long enough to treat them to a world-class eye roll as if he needed to remind his dad this wasn't his first time dealing with a protective mom and her pups.

"Ty, would you mind getting the luggage?" Sarah asked as she stepped from the vehicle. "I'm itching to visit the greenhouse. I'm sure Chris and Tim took good care of my plants."

"They worked with 'em whenever Emma didn't need them in the kitchen," Colt said, noting the same slight lift in Sarah's tone he'd heard the past three times she'd asked about the boys. He added a subtle hint of his own. "She taught 'em so much about cookin' an' such, I imagine they could 'bout take over."

"Uh-huh." Sarah squinted at the horizon, where the setting sun had turned low clouds into a sea of gold and pink. "For now, though, I'll need their help. The new plants should arrive the day after tomorrow. We have to make room for them."

"There's some other stuff you need to know." Prepared to dive into the topic he'd put off for as long as he could, Colt ran one hand over the brim of the new Stetson he'd picked up on his way through Okeechobee.

"Can we get to that in a bit?" Sarah flexed her fingers. "I can hardly wait to dig my hands into some good Florida dirt."

"Well, I…" But he was speaking to Sarah's back as the boss's wife headed for her beloved flowers. Watching her go, Colt resettled a hat that, like all the other changes in his life, was going to take some getting used to. He shrugged. "Guess I'll help with the luggage," he muttered. It was just as well. He could use the reprieve to get his wits about him.

While he and Ty pulled bags from the back of the truck, Colt took a slow, methodical survey of the parking area. He couldn't spot Emma's car and told himself that was a good thing, though, for the life of him, he wasn't sure how he'd survive the next five minutes, let alone the next five years, without her at his side. In her usual parking space sat a black sedan with an "I Heart Real Estate" sticker on the bumper. Evidently, Hank had made good time. Too good, in fact. Had something else brought his younger brother to the Circle P? Colt's brow furrowed. Weekly phone calls from his mom kept him updated on Arlene and the baby. At last report, the situation was still touch and go.

Suddenly in a hurry, he put his feet in motion. Seconds later, his boots rang against the wide steps leading into the ranch house. The front door swung open before Colt made it to the top, and his brother stepped onto the porch. Munching on a cookie, the younger Judd dusted a few crumbs onto the wide cedar planks.

"Hank." Colt dropped a pair of suitcases at the feet of a man who looked far too at ease to be the bearer of bad news. "You must've been halfway here when we spoke on the phone earlier," he said while they traded shakes and half hugs. "What's the hurry?"

"I'm just here for you, bro. It sounded like you were eager to hit the road." Hank held out a fistful of cookies. "Want one?"

Colt's stomach did a slow roll as he stared down at the treats he and Emma had baked for the Parkers' homecoming. He told himself the tremor that shot through him was just hunger. Earlier, he'd been in such a rush to put some much-needed distance between him and the woman he loved, he hadn't bothered to stop for lunch.

But the thin scab over his heartbreak was sure to re-open if Emma and Bree were still on the Circle P. "You haven't seen Emma, have you?"

"The cook?" Hank's eyes widened. "You know what she did, don't you?"

"Hey, Hank." Loaded down with luggage and bags, Ty brushed past. "Don't stand out here jawin'. Grab a bag and close the door." The Circle P's owner trudged to the bottom of the staircase, where he dropped a load of suitcases bearing red overweight tags. When Colt and Hank added theirs to the pile, Ty asked, "Are you going someplace, Colt?" He turned to Hank. "I didn't expect to see you here. And what did our cook do?"

"You haven't told 'em?" A grin spread across Hank's face. "The PBR made Colt a sweet deal if he'd quit loafin' around here and get back to work."

While Colt considered throttling his brother for the way he'd dropped the bomb, concern deepened the lines around Ty's mouth. "Is that true?"

His eyes on the doorway to the kitchen, Colt shrugged. "This isn't how I wanted you to find out, but yeah. I'm heading out tomorrow."

"Leaving the ranch in my capable hands." Hank, ever the salesman, stepped forward. "I may not be able to ride a bull as well as Colt, but I know as much about managing the Circle P as he does. And I'm not going anywhere till Royce and Randy get here."

Ty expelled air. "This isn't exactly the welcome home I expected, but it sounds like you've taken care of things. Now, what's this about our cook?"

A troubled look crossed Hank's face. His voice dropped to a stage whisper. "She's gone. Packed up—lock, stock and barrel—and hit the road. She didn't even stick around long enough to help with dinner tonight. Chris and Tim are doing the best they can, but…" He tsked. "Damn shame, if you ask me. These are the best cookies I ever tasted."

Gone. The relief Colt expected at not having to face Emma again never materialized. Instead, the bands across his chest tightened.

"Let me get this straight." Ty's voice dropped into a lower register. "You're leaving *and* we've lost our cook? Ever think those two items might qualify as an emergency?"

"I hear ya." Colt absorbed Ty's censure. His friend was right. Ty should have been kept in the loop. Would have been, except everything had happened so fast there hadn't been time to so much as make a phone call.

While Ty continued to glower, the front door eased open. Smiling, Sarah joined the trio in the great room.

"Hank! I didn't know you were here." After giving him a brief peck on the cheek, she turned to Colt. "The boys have done a marvelous job with the nursery. They even started an herb garden for our new cook. I need to thank them. Are they in the kit—" Noticing the grim faces around her, she stopped. "What's wrong?"

"Emma's gone," Hank blurted.

"Really?"

As one, the three men nodded.

"What a shame. I really liked her. I'm so sorry, Colt." A pensive frown crossed the redhead's brow. "Do you want to talk about it?"

Hank's eyes widened as understanding finally sank in. "Wait a minute." He stared at his brother. "You and Emma?"

Colt sliced the air with one hand. "Doesn't matter. She— I told you about the changes she made."

Some, like the coffeepot and fruit in the lunch bags, were obvious. Others, not so much. Like the ones she'd made in his heart, his life. She'd turned a nomadic cowboy into a man who craved nothing more than a quiet evening by the fireplace, his girl in his arms, his babies upstairs. That he couldn't have what he wanted, that was his own misery to bear.

He swallowed past a fresh burst of pain and steadied himself. He had to make Ty and Sarah understand why Emma had left.

"She…" Unwilling to let her shoulder the blame, he tried again. "There was an accident. In the kitchen. Most of the Circle P's cookbook was damaged. We spent the past month salvaging what we could and testing out new recipes to replace the ones that were lost. Emma's a good cook. A great one," he corrected. "We made a lot of progress. But then a four-star restaurant in Fort Lauderdale offered her better pay and the chance to make a name for herself. It was simply too good to pass up," he said, his words spilling out faster than the announcer's at the rodeo.

"Wait." Sarah held up a hand. "I'm confused. She had all that in New York. She came here to have more time with her daughter. So why'd she leave again?"

Knowing the time had come to explain his role in Emma's swift departure, Colt widened his stance. "Truth be told, she didn't want to take the job. But this kind of thing, it doesn't come along very often. So I—" he scuffed one boot against the floor "—I fired her."

When he managed to look up, three pairs of eyes stared at him as if he'd suddenly lost all his marbles.

"I had to," he protested. "Wait till you read the *Beaks and Wings* article. You'll see. Even they realized she was wasting her talents here."

Silence filled the room. Sarah's mouth opened and closed as though she'd started to say something, but thought better of it. Hank stared into the distance, unable to meet Colt's gaze. At last, Ty cleared his throat.

"Well, what's done is done." Slowly, Ty unclenched his hands at his sides. "We left you in charge of the Circle P while we were gone. We have to trust that you made the right decision."

Sarah glanced at her husband and nodded. She tapped one finger against her lower lip. "The cookbook, on the other hand, that's one problem I can solve." She disappeared into the office.

Listening to the sounds of drawers opening and closing, Colt shot a questioning gaze toward Ty. From the look on his face, the owner was as much in the dark as he was.

"Here." Sarah bustled into the room and pressed a tiny object into Colt's hand.

"What's this?"

"Do I have to spell it out for you, cowboy?" The slim redhead grinned up at him. "Computers were a big part of my job with DCF. You don't think I'd trust all our recipes to paper, do you?"

Colt stared down at a piece of plastic no bigger than a cricket. His thoughts stumbled, unable to absorb the idea that the tiny device held four generations worth of Circle P recipes. Or that it had been here through all the long nights he and Emma had spent together in the kitchen.

The irony of the situation struck him. He'd fallen in love with Emma while they tried to re-create the lost recipes, but they'd been here all along. A chuckle worked its way up from his middle. By the time it reached his chest, it bubbled into laughter. Before he knew it, he was holding his sides, tears streaming down his cheeks. He glanced up and caught his brother staring at him as if he had two heads. Ty and Sarah's quizzical expressions sobered him.

Seconds later, an altogether different emotion swept over him and he beat feet while he still could. He barely made it to his room before his legs gave out from under him. Slowly, he slid onto the floor, his back against the bed.

He slung one arm over his eyes. After all they'd been through, he had to tell Emma about the cookbook. He owed her that much. Not today, though. Not until he gave his aching heart some time to heal. Soon, though, very soon, he'd track her down in Fort Lauderdale. But he refused to kid himself. There'd be no happy reunion. He would simply deliver a message. Unless…

Was there any chance she'd take him back? He refused to fool himself. He'd hurt her, destroyed their love. If she'd give him a second chance, though, he'd spend the rest of his life making it up to her.

But if not, putting Hank to work finding him a place of his own wouldn't work. Not unless he had someone to share his hopes and dreams for the future. And he couldn't stay at the Circle P. His childhood home would never be his home again. Not without Emma. Which left the job with the PBR and, though he knew it was just a job and not a life, he figured it might be all he deserved.

Chapter Thirteen

"This is your office, Chef."

With a proud flourish, Paul, the owner of Marco Paulo's, stepped aside. Emma peered into a windowless room far smaller than the Circle P's pantry. Stacks of paperwork covered a built-in desk. Linens spilled from sample boxes piled in one corner. Hemmed in on all sides by three-by-five cards and Post-it notes, thumbtacks pinned a marked-up copy of the restaurant's standard menu to the wall.

Paul noted her intense study of a much-revised staffing diagram. He squeezed past the desk to rip the sheet from the wall. "We've had some turnovers of late," he offered. "You may hear a few complaints from those who expected a promotion from within. I'm sure you'll prove yourself in their eyes. Each of our cooks is brilliantly *creative*."

Her jaw clenched at the standard euphemism for *difficult*. So Marco Paulo's kitchen was a hotbed of jealousy and dissent, was it? A wave of homesickness for the Circle P's quiet atmosphere, where the only rustle was the sound of the breeze through tall grass, swept over her. She squared her shoulders. Dwelling on all she'd lost only made for more heartache.

"Perhaps your daughter should sit here while I intro-duce you to your staff."

Bathed in pasty light from the overhead fluorescent, Bree clung more tightly to her hand than the day they'd faced down alligators on the Circle P. Emma didn't have to glance down to know that Mrs. Wickles dragged on the floor at her daughter's side. She couldn't, she wouldn't, return to the days of dropping Bree off at day care before noon and leaving her with a sitter until after midnight. Despite all the responsibilities of her new job, she'd bring Bree to work with her. She'd clear a space for toys and coloring books. Wedge a cot into the min-iscule office. Turn the room into her daughter's home-away-from-home.

"She'll stay with me." She snugged the little girl closer.

"Suit yourself." Paul led the way past a kitchen where every inch of space performed double-duty. "I've asked everyone else to meet us in the dining room."

Seconds later, Emma told herself that, okay, maybe bringing her active four-year-old to work at Marco Paulo's wasn't such a great idea. The owner obviously thought black was, well, the new black. Black linens and plates adorned the tables in the dining room, where black draperies blocked every ray of sunlight. Even the staff dressed in black from head to toe. The few touches of color scattered about the room looked so strikingly out of place they actually hurt her eyes.

She brushed a hand down the front of her own chef's whites while she took a measured look at the predomi-nantly male assembly. Passed over for promotion, her new second-in-command leaned insolently against the wall. His deep scowl warned Emma to double-check every dish that left the kitchen lest he sabotage plates destined for important patrons. In the opposite corner, the pastry chef leaned a little too familiarly against the saucier while, from across the room, the fry cook—the apparent low man in a lover's triangle—glared at the couple. She moved on to the pantry chef, who clutched the keys he wore on a chain around his neck as if he'd refuse her request to see the larder. In between, junior cooks and assistants spread out according to an unfriendly pecking order.

Clearly, managing this kitchen would take as much tact and diplomacy as it did actual cooking skills. As for raising her daughter here, Emma shook her head. Try as she might, she couldn't imagine Bree growing up a healthy, well-adjusted child in such a hostile environment. She inhaled a breath that shook with longing for the easy camaraderie of the Circle P.

Another bridge burned, she told herself. Or, more appropriately, doused. Stiffening her spine, she drew her carry case out of her pocket. On the Circle P, she'd begun each day by giving Chris and Tim a short lesson in the culinary arts, a tradition she intended to carry forward into this new job. She'd even chosen her topic—the intricately carved strawberry roses she meant to install as her signature garnish.

Tha-pet-ah, tha-pet-ah. The cotton case filled with gleaming chef's knives unrolled on the table. She stared down at the tools by which she plied her trade. From them, she looked up into a dozen angry faces. Suddenly, her heart wasn't in it. As quickly as she'd opened her case, she rolled it up and tied it closed.

"As you were, chefs," she said, adapting the term

she'd heard far too often in her childhood home. "This isn't going to work."

She had to face facts. She couldn't submit Bree to this unfriendly atmosphere any more than she could stand it herself. She'd left her heart on the Circle P. Maybe she couldn't go back there. Maybe there wasn't another kitchen in the world exactly like it. But she didn't have to settle for this. For the hostility, the long hours, the oppressive heat. She wanted warmth from soft breezes blowing through a window overlooking a cow pasture, not the sweltering, chaotic atmosphere of a restaurant kitchen.

Paul turned as red as one of the beets in the house salad. "Chef, we open in—" sputtering, he glanced at his watch "—six hours."

"You'll have to do it without me." Paul's hand on her forearm slowed her. At a deep growl from somewhere behind her, the man flinched away as if he'd been bitten.

Emma's heart thudded an extra beat. She knew that sound. Almost afraid to breathe, to look, she pivoted slowly. Framed in the open doorway stood the imposing figure of Colt Judd, the one man she'd never expected to see again. Her traitorous heart broke into a staccato rhythm.

"Mr. Colt!" Bree broke free. Making a beeline for him, she clambered over a chair and fairly launched herself into his arms. "Did you bring Chocolate?"

Colt lifted the girl high and hugged her close. He ruffled Bree's hair. "No, sweetheart. He's too little to be this far away from his mama."

"That's what Mommy said. But I miss him." Bree curled her little arms around Colt's neck. She rested her head on his shoulder and sighed.

Tears stung Emma's eyes, but she mustered a firm, "Let's go." She swept past, her head held as high as her throbbing heart would allow. Figuring Marco Paulo's staff had heard enough of her personal life, she led the way through the cramped kitchen, down the hall and out the door into the alley.

Carrying the stench of rotted food, a heavy blanket of heat and humidity slapped her in the face. Her feet stuttered to a halt. She scanned the dark passage and the blinding sunshine that lay beyond. Where now? She had no home, no job, no future.

"I know a place." Colt shifted Bree to one hip. "It's not far."

Her head full of questions she refused to ask, Emma put her feet in motion behind Colt's. A short walk along Fort Lauderdale's tree-lined Riverwalk took them to a gazebo set among lush tropical plants. Built to resemble a cupcake, the pink-and-white setting looked far too romantic for goodbyes, and the tiniest drop of hope that Colt had come to whisk her home to the Circle P landed in her chest. She wiped it away. Instead, she stared at the river that lapped gently against a peach-colored breakwater while she gave herself a stern talking-to. By choosing the PBR over her, Colt had stomped on her dreams of home and forever and family. So why had he trailed her to Fort Lauderdale?

"Mommy, can I look at the water?" Bree scrambled from Colt's arms.

"Is it safe?" Emma hesitated.

"It's fine," Colt answered. "She won't be out of my sight for a second."

When they met hers, his blue eyes ignited a flame under her broken heart. She drew in an unsteady breath when he tore his gaze away long enough to tell Bree to stay on the safe side of a wide coquina border.

"Did I hear right back there? You're walking away from Marco Paulo's?"

Her hands grasping the gazebo's sturdy rail for support, she met Colt's probing gaze. "Life's too short to waste it doing the things I don't want to do. Bree's growing up. Soon, she'll be in kindergarten, and then elementary school. I can't spend this time away from her, and Marco Paulo's is no place to raise a child."

"Any chance you'd consider coming back to the Circle P?"

"You fired me, Colt." Her breath hitched. Colt hadn't said *he* wanted her there, and why would he? He wasn't sticking around. He was leaving. Her resolve firmed, she focused on unfinished business. "Why are you here?"

Colt took a thick roll of paper from his back pocket. "Turns out, you and Sarah were on the same wavelength. She had every one of the Circle P's recipes stored on her computer. She said to give you this copy."

He thrust it into her hands. Relief flooded her chest as she gazed down at the pages that fluttered in the midmorning breeze. The recipes had been saved, after all. Did that mean she'd wasted time trying to re-create them with Colt? She glanced up at the tall rancher and knew, despite her broken heart, she wouldn't have traded a moment of it.

"Thanks," she whispered.

Colt stared over her head. "Ty and Sarah were miffed when you weren't there for their homecoming. Jimmy misses Bree and wants her to come back. They all do. As quick as you can."

She imagined creeping down the stairs to put the coffee on in the mornings and not being able to share a cup with Colt. Serving meals he hadn't taste tested. Roaming the house alone in the middle of the night because he wasn't there to put her troubles to rest. Slowly, she shook her head.

"No," she said, her voice a soft sigh. Blinking rapidly, she spared a quick glance at Bree. Her daughter stood far from the river's edge, tossing pebbles into the water. "I'll find another ranch, another place. Somewhere that doesn't hold...so many memories."

"I'm sorry I let you go. Sorrier than you could ever imagine. Won't you think about coming back?" Colt's blue eyes sought hers. "Will you come back...to me?"

A gust of wind muffled the last part of his sentence. Certain she hadn't heard him correctly, she drew in a breath that was far too unsteady for the words he was forcing her to say. She squared her shoulders, her voice a mere whisper. "I don't think I could stand it without you there."

Colt's brows knitted. He stepped closer, invading her space, herding her toward the wall of the gazebo. "What if I changed my mind? What if I stayed?"

Her breath caught in her throat as she tried to understand what she was hearing.

"I'm not going anywhere," he said rather emphatically. "I turned down the PBR's offer. The only reason I considered it in the first place was to let you have a chance at the kind of success you deserve."

Despite a pulse rate that rocketed toward the stars, she held her place. "Bree showed me your bags. She said it was a secret."

"She's four," Colt insisted. "Are you really going to leave over something a preschooler said?"

Not leaving. Her heart staggered beneath the weight of what she was hearing.

Colt moved marginally closer. "She was right about one thing. I am moving. To the little house. Now that Ty and Sarah are home, I thought it'd be best." His shirt stretched across his chest as he took a breath. "I was actually kind of hoping you'd move there with me. You and Bree."

Her heart stopped. "You want me and Bree..." Her voice trailed into nothingness.

"Not forever." He held up a hand, shushing her when her face fell. "Just until I can buy a piece of land, build us a real house. One with lots of space, a huge kitchen." He grinned. "I'll tell Hank to start looking for someplace close by. But I'm gonna need a cook..."

"What a coincidence." She summoned a tremulous version of her sauciest smile. "I happen to know one who's available."

Laughter sparked in Colt's eyes. He closed the gap between them. "I don't know." He frowned, teasing. "I'm kind of hard to please."

With that, Emma moved into his arms. "What kind of terms are you offering, cowboy?"

"I'll need a lifetime contract. I won't take anything less. They tell me I'm a hard, demanding man. It would take someone special, someone I loved with all my heart, to fill the position."

"Mmm." Emma pretended to give his offer some serious thought. "I think I can go for that. I'm head over heels in love with a rancher." She tipped her head, expecting the press of his lips against hers. Instead, he backed out of her arms, out of her embrace.

On bended knee, he drew a small box from his pocket

and said the words she'd longed to hear ever since she first glimpsed him on the front porch of the ranch house.

"Emma Shane, I'd be honored if you'd do me the favor of becoming my wife."

"Yes," she whispered. "Oh, yes." Tears stung her eyes.

At her quiet cry, Colt slipped a ring on the fourth finger of her left hand. The diamond flashed like fire when it caught the sun's golden rays. Colt stood, but before he could sweep her into his arms, Bree tugged on the hem of Emma's white coat.

"Mommy, Mr. Colt, what's going on? What'cha doing?"

Emma placed one hand over her heart as Colt leaned down to her daughter.

"I asked your mommy to marry me. She said yes," he answered. "But I have one more question." The heart-shaped locket he slipped from his pocket hung on a simple gold chain. "Will you be my little girl?" he asked Bree. "Forever and ever?"

Bree stared up at him. "Can I have Chocolate?"

"What would a ranch be without a dog or two?" Taking her response for an answer, he fixed the clasp around Bree's neck.

Emma smiled up at him as Colt slipped an arm around her waist while Bree studied her new necklace. When the little girl looked up, Emma held her breath. Her heart leaped into her throat as her daughter dropped to one knee in a perfect imitation of Colt's pose.

Her little voice filled with hope, Bree asked, "Will you be my daddy?"

Emma choked back tears, but she wasn't the only one. Moisture glistened in Colt's eyes, too, as he said words that, not so long ago, she'd never dreamed she'd hear.

"Forever and ever."

She was still brushing tears from her eyes when Colt's mouth claimed hers. The kiss to seal the deal didn't last long enough or go deep enough before she felt his lips curve into a smile. They drew apart to the scattered applause of passersby who'd glimpsed his proposal and stopped to watch. Pulling Bree into a group hug, Emma leaned into Colt's embrace, knowing they'd pick up where they'd left off once they were back home on the Circle P, where she'd found happiness and forever in the arms of her Glades County cowboy.

* * * * *

COMING NEXT MONTH FROM

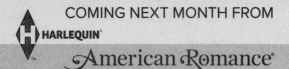

HARLEQUIN

American Romance®

Available June 3, 2014

#1501 HER COWBOY HERO
The Colorado Cades
by Tanya Michaels
When Colin Cade gets a job on Hannah Shaw's ranch, he doesn't expect her to be so young and beautiful—or to have a little boy who reminds Colin of the one he lost.

#1502 THE TEXAN'S BABY
Texas Rodeo Barons
by Donna Alward
In the first book of a new six-book miniseries, Lizzie Baron feels the need to let loose—and she gets help from Christopher Miller, a sexy saddle bronc rider. But their night together leads to an unexpected result!

#1503 THE SEAL'S BABY
Operation: Family
by Laura Marie Altom
Libby Dewitt, pregnant and alone, brings out the hero in Navy SEAL Heath Stone. But can Libby help him overcome his tragic past and love again?

#1504 A RANCHER'S HONOR
Prosperity, Montana
by Ann Roth
It was only supposed to be one night of fun—after all, day care owner Lana Carpenter and rancher Sly Pettit have nothing in common. Until they discover a connection between them they never could have imagined...

HARCNM0514

Lizzie Baron pressed the buzzer.

There was a click and then a voice. "Hello?"

"Uh…hi. I'm looking for Christopher Miller?"

"That's me."

"It's…uh…" She scrambled to think of what she'd said to him that night. "It's Elizabeth."

There was a pause.

"From the bar in Fort Worth."

The words came out strained.

"Come on up."

She could do this. She paused as she got off the elevator.

A door opened and Christopher stepped into the hall. Her feet halted and she stared at him, her practiced words flying out of her head.

He was staring at her, too. "It really is you," he said. "What the hell are you doing here?"

For weeks, Chris had been wondering if he should try to find out who she was. They'd met at a honky-tonk after a less-than-stellar rodeo performance on his part. He'd figured he'd nurse his wounds with a beer and head back to the motel where he was staying.

And then he'd seen her. He'd ordered another beer, looked over at her and she'd smiled, and all his brain cells turned to mush.

When he'd woken the next morning, the bed had been empty. That had been nearly two months ago.

"Elizabeth." He stepped aside so she could enter his apartment.

"Call me Lizzie. Everybody does."

"You didn't say your name was Lizzie the night we met."

"I was trying to be mysterious."

"It worked." He put his hands in his pockets. "How did you find me?"

"Rodeo's a small world."

"You're saying that you got my address from rodeo records?"

The blush was back. "Yes."

"Why would you do that?"

"Because I need to talk to you."

Quiet settled through the condo. Whatever she wanted to tell him, she was nervous. Afraid.

And then it hit him upside the head. "Look, do I need to be tested for an STD or something? Is that why you're here?"

"What the hell would give you that idea?"

"Hey, you're the one who disappeared and only gave me your first name. Now you show up weeks later, looking completely different, and say you need to talk to me. If it's not an STD, what the hell…"

His mouth dropped open.

"No," he whispered. "No, it isn't possible. We used condoms."

She looked up, misery etched in every feature. "I assure you it is possible. I'm pregnant, and the baby's yours."

Look for THE TEXAN'S BABY
by Donna Alward in June 2014
wherever books and ebooks are sold.

American Romance

He's just the hired help…

What kind of a cockeyed Pollyanna is Colin Cade working for? Her porch is rotting, her "guest cabin" is cheerless, and her land and livestock have only a geriatric cowboy to care for them. Yet Hannah Shaw is positive she can turn her ranch into a successful B and B—and that Colin's the man to make it happen.

But Colin can't stick around. He lives with the loss of his family by avoiding the memories, and the way he feels around Hannah and her young son is like a knife to the heart. Trouble is, he's better at ignoring his own pain than someone else's, and bright, cheerful Hannah has a heart as haunted as his own. She deserves to be happy—but maybe not with him….

Look for
Her Cowboy Hero
from *The Colorado Cades* miniseries

by TANYA MICHAELS

from Harlequin® American Romance®
Available June 2014
wherever books and ebooks are sold

Also available from *The Colorado Cades* miniseries
by Tanya Michaels:

Her Secret, His Baby
Second Chance Christmas